A DANCE THROUGH TIME

C000098588

BY J.P. REEDMAN

Copyright, JANUARY 2018
(Originally published, in part, as 'Elvingstone')

"Are you going to be all right?" James Thomas dropped the rusted old keys into Isabella Lawrence's outstretched hand. "It's not in the best part of town, and the weather forecast is awful. Mighty be a bit eerie too, hanging about in a mouldering old theatre."

"Maybe I'll photograph a ghost," mocked Isabella, thrusting the keys into her pocket. "If I do, I'm off to the papers tomorrow to get rich."

"Seriously," said James. He was a tall young man, suited, studious with slicked back hair and thin-rimmed glasses. "I really am a bit worried about the whole thing."

Isabella shrugged. "Don't be. I've crept around old castles in the dead of night using infrared film, and look, all in one piece. I shan't be too long, I promise. The keys will be back with you in an hour or two."

Turning, she left the estate agents and walked on to her car. Isabella was a photographer who specialised in architectural photos to be used in the restoration of historic buildings. '*Cracked plaster is my specialty*', she used to tell those who imagined she spent her days shooting portraits of gurgling babies, badly behaved brats, and the occasional family dog.

Flicking on the Sat Nav in the car, she let its robotic voice direct her towards London's East End. The Tower flashed by, lit up already, for it was late September and the nights were just starting to draw in. Its turrets glowed yellow-pale against a hard black sky; the moon was a thin crescent hanging above. Next to it, Tower Bridge glowed green and pale, almost more sinister than the ancient castle itself, looming in the dark like some fantasy prop from a film.

Then both vanished behind her, and the roads closed in, full of dark, lightless buildings. As she drove, mindful of the droning voice on her Satnav, Isabella realised it was getting foggy outside the car window. Streetlights, red, amber and green, blinked fitfully in the hazy whiteness. "Damn!" she spat. This weather wasn't making her job easier. She'd been told the little old streets around the derelict theatre were hard to navigate at the best of times.

The fog grew thicker, wrapping lampposts and houses. "A real pea-souper," she murmured, although she knew it wasn't—the London Fogs famous in old-time movies were long gone—they vanished with the cessation of the use of coal in fireplaces. This obscuration was just plain old fog from the river brought on by fluctuating temperature.

"You have come to 191 Lord Alley, on your right!" The metallic voice from the Sat Nav intoned.

Isabella glanced out of the window. A parking place on the roadside, up against the curb. Convenient. Pulling in, she leapt from her Ford Fiesta and went to the boot to grab her photography kit. As she picked up the heavy bag, she glanced around her. The neighbourhood had a slightly dodgy reputation, as James had warned her, but it seemed quiet tonight. Almost unusually so.

2

She could scarcely even hear the sounds of the city—the endless traffic, the sirens, the deep underground rumble from the tube. Maybe it was the fog.

For an unknown reason, a little shiver rippled down her spine. It was as if she were caught in a strange fog-bound bubble, in London…and yet not a part of it. At least not the London she knew…

"Don't be asinine," she murmured to herself, as she locked the car and shoved her keys into her pocket. "So what if it's abnormally quiet? Better chance you won't get back and find all the wheels taken off your car."

She began to walk down Lord Alley, which lay on her left. The street was cobbled; her heels made dull clopping noises like the hooves of a horse. On her right stood a high brick wall, bordering a decayed and boarded-up factory. Glass used as a burglar deterrent glittered along the top of the wall. Unfriendly, decidedly so.

Isabella continued to walk. The houses on the opposite side to the factory all looked empty. Not one light shone in any window. Surprising—for there had been much redevelopment going on in recent years. In fact, that's why she was going to photograph the old Queen's Head Theatre, to pass the results on to heritage bodies who would decide what could be done by potential buyers and to give guidance to would-be restorers.

Suddenly a building front, bigger than all the others, loomed up before her. Boarded windows massed with peeling old flyers, a broad door covered in graffiti. The porch had two pillars reaching up to support a scallop-shaped roof, and across the front was written THE QUEEN'S HEAD.

"So this must be it," murmured Isabella. "Looks like a set from a horror film."

At that moment, she heard a rustling noise away in the swirling tendrils of the fog. She jumped nervously. Glancing over her shoulder, she thought she saw, for a brief, unnerving instant, a tall figure wearing what seemed to be a large top hat. The figure stood as still as stone; she felt as if unseen eyes bored into her. She was reminded all too well that this was Jack the Ripper's old patch, and even though that sadistic criminal was long dead, there was always some oddball out there seeking to emulate his gory 'hero.' Copycat killers…or, more likely, a sick prankster…

"It's probably just a prank. Or someone taking a ghost walk," she mumbled, trying to calm her nerves. It didn't really work. A needle of fear stabbed into her and she felt hair rise on the back of her neck. She should have taken up James' offer to come with her on the shoot…

Fingers trembling she fumbled with the theatre's keys in her pocket. They felt icy against her palm. Bringing them out, she thrust the one with a tag that said 'Main' into the rusty lock, turned it. Nothing happened. "Shit!" she swore. She glanced over her shoulder. The mist has deepened, and once again, she felt a presence. Drawing nearer. No one was visible though…the mist was too thick…

She tried the key again; twisting it and leaning against the door to try to force the unwilling old lock. A trickle of red rust ran from the keyhole, streaking down like a tendril of blood—an image that she certainly did not savour, and then with a loud clunk, the key turned properly and the door glided open.

Isabella stumbled into the foyer and slammed the door behind her, quickly relocking it from inside. It was pitch-black in the Queen's Head and smelt of damp and rot. It was nearly as unwelcoming as the alley outside—her imagination went wild, thinking of what could lie in the blackness beyond.

Nervously, her hand went out, feeling along the walls. There were electric lights; she had looked up their positions on old diagrams before she'd left the office for the shoot. The theatre itself dated from 1750, but it had continued in use until the 1980's, when it had been 'Joker's Nightclub', so it had a few modern amenities such as electricity.

After what seemed an eternity of searching in the dark, her hand fell on what was clearly a light switch. Now, just pray the lights still worked! Biting her lip, she flipped the switch and with a dull, dank sizzle the lights throughout the theatre fluttered to life.

She was standing in the lobby. All the old 80's furniture from Joker's lay piled up here, under ragged dustsheets, forgotten and unwanted. The head of a Joker from a pack of cards gleamed out from an electronic display above what had been the box office. Underfoot red carpets bunched in soggy, wet rolls. Clumps of plaster lay on the floor and peeled from the walls.

It was a weird and atmospheric place, but the lobby, half 80's kitsch, part Victorian and part Georgian, wasn't what Isabella was looking for. Once a buyer had acquired the building, the 80's décor would be ripped out and proper restorations begun to return it to its dignified glory. The nightclub and its uncaring, trendy owners had ruined both lobby and bar area with renovations, but reportedly had left the main theatre almost intact, bar the seats, which were apparently mouldering in storage in the cellars.

A little more confident, with lights on and the door firmly locked behind her, Isabella shouldered her camera bag and headed for what had once been the stalls. Pushing aside two swinging doors covered by glow-in-the-dark stars that had stopped glowing around 1990, she entered the theatre auditorium. The frayed ends of red curtain, hanging down behind the door, slid over her face like spider webs.

The auditorium was a renovator's dream. The now-chairless floor, where discos had taken place at Joker's, swept down towards a long, low stage fronted by an orchestra pit. Across the wide proscenium arch danced a row of carved cherubs, twined with a garland of flowers; once brightly gilded, their paint had partly chipped away, leaving patterns of light and darkness. The vast heavy stage curtains had been pulled back and secured by ropes; dark blue velvet fringed by tassels of gold, they hung from ceiling to floor.

Isabella turned in a circle, gaze scanning the place. There were empty theatre boxes, their fronts patched with faded gilding, supported by columns carved with theatrical masks—Tragedy and Comedy. Toward the back of the theatre, high in the Gods, there were alcoves where folk had once gathered during intermission; the niches bore murals of Greeks maidens in flowing gowns, carrying baskets of grapes on their shoulders. The paintings were badly damaged, cracked and stained by some leakage from the ceiling, and one had a profanity scrawled over her exposed breast…but they were clearly painted by a highly-skilled artist of long ago.

"This is going to be better than I hoped," murmured Isabella, drawing down the zip on her camera bag and bringing out her SLR. Climbing the creaking stairs at the end of the hall, she began to take detailed close ups of the murals, then, adjusting the aperture and using a splintered handrail as a makeshift tripod, took some slow shutter shots down towards the stage.

"I wonder what it was like to dance out there, long ago." Isabella focussed, trying to get the dust cloud illuminated by the thin beam of the old lamp on the wall. "In front of an audience, in front of the wealthy of the day. Huh, not wonderful, probably…didn't they think actresses were hardly better than prostitutes back then?"

The camera shutter whirred. Isabella smiled to herself. She was certain she had some cracking shots…

Suddenly a floorboard creaked behind her. She jumped, clutching the camera against her chest. Jesus…what was…

Nothing….

She turned around, scanning the doorways with worried eyes.

Nothing.

Just old floorboards almost ready to give way. The restorers would need to get someone on that job right away before the flooring fell in and made their job even harder.

She approached the stage and began photographing the proscenium arch, the carving on the woodwork. Smiles and weeping faces filled the frames.

And then she heard it…louder now. A footstep.

It was obvious what it was this time—firm and determined. The sound of a foot in a heavy boot striking the wooden floor.

Her heart began to hammer. Rushing away from the ominous sound toward the stage, she flung herself up the stairs at the side and ran out across the dusty boards. Breathing heavily, she stared out across the auditorium.

Again, nothing…

Then the pale yellow lights in their sconces started dimming, sizzling as they dulled towards darkness. A shadow moved, stretched out across the floor. "Arabella…" whispered a voice, an echoing voice. *Arabella…*

"Whoever you are, keep back!" cried Isabella. She grasped her car keys, remembering that they could be used as weapons. One jab to the eye could give a nasty injury. "My friend is waiting outside; he will be coming to check on me any minute."

The shadow, embraced by the other deepening shadows in the theatre, did not move. Did not respond. The presence remained however, mysterious, sinister with its overtones of the unknown. The hall was getting darker as the lights failed, going out one by one with a sudden and disconcerting popping noise.

Isabella began to sweat. She dared not run down through the auditorium toward the doors leading to the lobby; for that that was where the shadows lay thickest, where she'd heard that heavy, ominous tread. Backstage was no good either; she'd already been informed the old stage door had been bricked in decades ago. There was a fire escape on her right hand side, approximately twenty yards away…perhaps that was her best hope.

Her only hope.

Camera grasped in her hand, she began to run, and at the same time the shadows swirled and a man became visible—the tall man in the top hat and long, swirling, Victorian cape…

Isabella gasped in shock and fear…and at that moment, the rotten floorboards of the stage gave way beneath her feet and she tumbled down into the darkness below.

Her head struck something hard in the gloom, a sharp pain lanced through her skull, and then she fell still.

Isabella awoke with a figure looming over her. She started in fear then saw that it was a pale-faced girl in a stage costume comprised of ruffled tulle and fairy wings. "Arabella!" She shook her shoulder. "Arabella, are you not well? What's wrong? Is your corset too tight? Did you faint?"

The girl leaned over, trying to help Isabella into a sitting position. "Arabella, you're so white? Please speak to me. We're due on stage soon… You…you're not with child or anything bad like that are you?"

The strange girl was asking if she was *pregnant*. The question brought Isabella to full wakefulness. "Of…of course not!" *And why are you calling me ARAbella and not ISAbella*, she thought nervously. *Is this some kind of a sick joke?*

"Come on, then…we haven't much time!"

The girl grabbed Isabella's hands and pulled her to her feet, guiding her through a warren of tunnels offset by rooms—dressing rooms, prop rooms, wardrobe rooms. As dark as it had been when Isabella entered the Queen's Head, now there was plenty of light—lanterns holding candles bucked merrily on black iron hooks along the sweating walls.

For the first time, Isabella noticed she wasn't wearing her normal jeans and t-shirt. An awful start of sick fear ran through her. She was in a costume similar to the other girl who clutched her hand. An old-fashioned dance costume, she presumed. And yes, she was wearing a very tight corset that almost took her breath away. How could such madness be possible? Someone had to have had her…or his…dirty hands on her. She shuddered at the thought.

As soon as she managed to see an exit, she was out and running for the nearest police station.

Somewhere in the theatre, music began to play, vibrating through the wall beside her. Isabella jumped in fright again—it sounded like a full orchestra was playing. But there had been no one in the building when she'd come in; just herself…and her stalker.

"We must hurry," said her companion insistently. "Our dance number is almost ready to begin."

Dance number. Isabella shook her head dumbly. Like many little girls, she'd wanted to be a ballerina when she was about six. She'd taken a few lesson with the local dance school under Ms Tatanya Bareva (real name Joan Lumb from Hull), a pouting and precise woman who spoke with a put on Russian accents and who wore a tight chignon that forced her plucked brows up into devilish points, which she thought gave her an aristocratic—or autocratic—air. Isabella had done well enough under Ms Bareva's stern tutelage ...till the day she was knocked off her bike by a joy-rider, shattering her leg in two places and messing up the cartilage in her knee. Ms Bareva had sadly shaken her head when she'd finally returned to lessons. "I do not think you will dance again. Not professionally anyway."

"I...I can't do this..." Isabella hissed to the girl next to her.

"Whatever are you on about? Have you suddenly acquired stage fright? We only have a few more performances before we are done with this terrible production! Now...go on with you, before we miss our cues!"

The dark corridor ended. Isabella could see a stage...the very one she had fallen though. But there was no sign of damage to the boards, and the stage was brightly lit. And the empty auditorium...it was full. Of seats. And people. People who appeared to be in fancy dress—top hats and tails, huge hats with ribbons and lace, grand silk gowns with bustles.

More and more, Isabella began to think this was some kind of a set up. But yet she had definitely fallen, and lost consciousness...and they'd taken her clothes. Sweat beaded on her forehead. What if she had been taken prisoner by some perverse secret society who...who maybe had terrible things waiting in store during her 'performance'...

The lights on the stage dimmed and changed to forest-green. The little fair-haired girl gave Isabella a push between the shoulderblades. A floodlight hit her eyes, near blinding her.

And then she was dancing...It was like something from the old classic film *THE RED SHOES*, where the shoes would not cease their dance. Her feet were moving as if guided by unseen forces, graceful and strong. Isabella twirled, the white tulle of her gown billowing about her. Around her, other dancers leapt and pirouetted—crows in black, feathered cloaks, rustling in the wind of their speed, green-hatted pixies that frolicked and gambolled in long-toed shoes, and flower-maidens with daisy-chain hair and great gold sunflowers strapped to their backs.

I can't be dancing! she thought frantically. *I haven't danced for years. And my leg! My wrecked leg!* She stared down as she whirled around the stage in the milling sea of her fellows. Her hem blew up, rippling in the wind of her speed, and she gasped—two big red scars had marred her right leg since girlhood. They were a source of constant embarrassment; when swimming she covered them with special makeup. Now, they were GONE.

"I am going to wake up in a minute," she whispered to herself.

The half-belief that the dance was merely a dream gave her a certain confidence. She wasn't a prisoner; she was just caught in what...a lucid dream? Why not go with it until she awoke? She *would* finally awake, and then everything would be normal.

She threw herself into the dance, immersing herself in the music, pirouetting and twirling the papier-mâché sunflower pinned to her frothy gown. Strange little memories entered her mind...memories that were not her own. A childhood cottage...horses and carts...the name 'Arabella'. Arabella Lorne, Isabella Lawrence, the thoughts and memories of Isabella...and of someone else...blended until they melded together, interlocked, inseparable forever more. Isabella now knew everything. In this world, she was Arabella, while the girl who escorted her to the stage was her roommate Effie, and she was a jobbing (and struggling) actress and dancer...

And it was 1838...

I must be going mad... she thought, but then even that thought receded from her mind.

The dance was all that mattered....well, not *quite* all.

There was the man in the viewing box up by the balcony.

Him. The one who attended every performance. Her admirer. With a shock, Isabella realised she knew him. The top-hatted shadowy figure that had followed her from the alley into the theatre...*Who followed through a locked door*...

Tiptoeing lightly, Isabella danced out along the edge of the stage, deliberately losing her sunflower, which was hustled to the wings by one of the pixies. This was the high point of her performance, her one chance to shine separately from the rest. She was now the sad and tragic sprite of the weeping willow, tossing her hair back and forth, back and forth, as she mourned a faithless lover. Through strands of showering hair, she allowed her gaze to wander upwards from the half-empty stalls to the even emptier balcony, to the Gods high above...and then to the boxes on stage right.

She took in the faded decor of the old theatre, tired even in 1838, it seemed—the rococo ceiling flecked with gold paint, the plump Greek ladies with their grapes, the theatrical masks that gazed out of a haze of bronze knotwork on balcony and wall.

But, then her gaze wandered. To the man. The admirer.

He was seated, as was usual, in the nearest box, wearing a dark cravat and his customary tall hat, his bearing upright and almost stiff as he watched the show. She tried to get a good look at him, although it was difficult with the stage lights dazzling her eyes, making blobs of the figures in the audience. From what she could make out, he was upright, youthful, and dark-haired, his face a white blur in the shadows.

He had come every night since the show had opened, a rich man as evidenced by the carriage that brought him to the theatre door, but mysterious, his presence unannounced, and without friends of attendants in either carriage or box. After the show, he had sent gifts to Arabella Lorne's dreary shared dressing room—bouquets of meadow flowers plucked far from the city, an antique compact set with lapis lazuli, a rose-red silk scarf with bronze tassels that smelled of an old rich perfume. Yet, despite his generosity, he had never waited for her to exit the theatre or requested that they meet….

Isabella's cheeks began to burn. The man was staring down at her, she sensed it, his unsmiling, impassive gaze stabbing her like a sword. Why? *Why?* What significance did her have for her…or that other part of her that seemed to be a young actress called Arabella?

She mulled through Arabella's memories and thoughts, jumbled in her mind like fragments of brightly-coloured glass. Arabella was as perplexed as she. Many of the chorus girls had 'admirers' but mostly these admirers were sad old men looking for mistresses, for young bright things to convince them they were still virile. They believed actresses and dancers, pretty girls but mostly poor, were easy pickings. Many were. Arabella, however, was not, and she had sent no encouragement to the white-faced young man, nor had she acknowledged his gifts—she could not, even had she wished to, for once they were delivered to Old Crump, the stage doorman, her secret 'admirer' always leapt into his carriage and galloped into the night with a crack of whips and a thunder of carriage wheels…

Isabella (or was it Arabella?) decided to dwell no more on the unsettling man in the box. He was only a temporary distraction, whoever he might be. Soon he would be out of Arabella's life forever…the show at Queen's Head had only three more days left to run—and thank goodness for that, as the attendance had dwindled to a handful of theatre diehards. Cast and crew were unhappy and argumentative, and there were rumours no one would receive their full pay. If the latter were true, Arabella would have to bribe Mrs Gold, the proprietor of the boarding house where she roomed, to allow her to stay on with rent in arrears till she found another job. Well, the admirer's gifts might prove useful as a bit of bribery; dull, bitter old Mrs Gold like a bit of glitter on the sly.

Determined to return to concentrating on her performance, Isabella pirouetted her way further back onto the stage, where a ring of Pixies circled her, chanting, "Who now sees the faery queen? Where is she, fair and serene…"

Isabella's gaze darted to the corridor on stage left where the stage manager was standing in the shadows, the set of his shoulders clearly showing tension and strain. He saw her look and shrugged hopelessly. Where was the 'faery queen,' indeed? Arabella's thoughts flashed up, in a moment of panic that almost stopped Isabella's dancing feet. The Diva Eulalia Fairbanks should have been waiting in the wings for her grand entrance in the show's glittering finale…

Eulalia had clearly missed her cue—again. Such behaviour happened almost weekly these days. No doubt, she had been throwing a tantrum in her dressing room, driven to near-madness by a crack in her heavy stage makeup or by the tightness of a gown that no longer fit her expanding figure…

Down in the orchestra pit, Isabella could see the vague outline of the conductor standing on his small podium. He glanced up and the lights illuminated his worried face. A bead of perspiration popped out on his brow, a shimmering gem that slid down his face and hung suspended from his chin. He motioned to the musicians to repeat the last refrain and hopefully keep the audience from realising that something was amiss.

There was a rumble from backstage. A curse muffled by the swelling music. A bright flood lamp burst into life, dry ice-fog rose in a cloud…and then she was there, Madam Eulalia Fairbanks, ageing diva, one-time court favourite, as the Faery Queen. Her soprano voice reached for the rafters in a series of high-pitched ululations as she swept out onto the boards, waving plump hands in melodramatic motions—a cover for the fact that she could no longer make such moves with her body or her feet.

 Crimson gown straining at its sequined seams, Eulalia possessed the stage with the power of a storm. Black, curled hair towered high on her head, twisted with ornate wires bearing faux gems that glittered as the lights struck them. Her face was a pallid mask, with strong, attractive features, most particularly the huge, expressive dark eyes beneath slashes of iridescent green stage paint…but the chin had grown double, and deep lines had formed from nose to mouth.

Undulating like a red serpent, she drew a stage dagger from her belt and waved it above her head in a menacing fashion, catching the gas-lamps' light along the edges of the blade. The knife, in truth, could not cut butter but a gasp came from the meagre audience; they, at least, were willing to suspend disbelief.

Eulalia Fairbanks, mistress of the stage, singer extraordinaire, was this night Titania, the Faerie Queen, in the rather unsuccessful operetta, The Titan's Fall, by one Mr Harold Mason, Esquire. The lack of box office appeal had fallen squarely on to Mason's shoulders, with Eulalia's manager, George Huxtable, thundering to the press about how his client had been duped into an accepting a dubious role of little merit, written by a hack living on the dregs of an inheritance and fancying himself an author.

Arabella Lorne knew the official story was not in any way the truth. She had heard Eulalia shrieking at Huxtable through the thin walls of the dressing room that she, the great Diva, was finished, washed up, old hat, reduced to taking any role she was offered…and to add to her distress, she had not managed to snare a prince or man of means. And it was unlikely she ever would because she was over forty and growing stout and ugly. The tirade ended with bawling, crying, the smashing of teacups and wine bottles, and even the occasional mirror…

Isabella pressed her hand to her mouth, suppressing a giggle at Arabella's unflattering memories of the Diva. She caught her 'friend', the girl Effie, casting her a strange look and shaking her head. "What are you doing?" Effie mouthed.

 Losing a moment's concentration, Isabella suddenly stepped too far to the right and almost stumbled into Eulalia. The Primadonna's deep brown eyes flashed enraged fire. "Bitch!" she mouthed, painted lips arching into a red moue. She waved her stage dagger even more fiercely, warning Isabella to get out of her spotlight.

Recovering her equilibrium, Isabella danced away into the darkness near the stage left exit. She could see her fellow chorus members staring at her, aware of her blunder. Effie looked thunderstruck.

Eulalia, taking centre stage, was ramping up her performance for the grand finale. Deserted by Oberon, the inflamed Titania was about to end her thousand- year-long life by stabbing herself in the heart with a magic dagger tempered in Dragon's bile that would wrest away her immortality. Eulalia huffed and heaved, her top of her huge bosom, pushed up by a heavily-boned corset, spilling immodestly out of the low-cut neckline of her gown. Her voice ascended in a warbling wail that shook the theatre's chandeliers…but the notes were a little flat, making her vocals resemble a harpy's shriek rather than the death-cry of an ancient being so stricken by loss that death was preferable to an empty immortality.

Isabella grimaced a little at the strident sound. Ear-splitting. Next to her, in the shadows, Effie Blunt, one of the other flower-maids, elbowed her lightly in the ribs. "Arabella, for goodness sake, what's got into you tonight? It's like you're possessed!"

On the stage, the fake dagger flashed down; the audience, a sea of bobbing blackish faces, shifted like an army of half-materialised ghosts. Eulalia clutched the stage knife to her breast, releasing a vial full of cow's blood secreted in the lace gathered at her neck. Redness spattered the Diva's crepey skin, splotching darker red across the satin of her gown.

The crowd gasped. Titania's death scene in The Titan's Fall was a rather lurid spectacle, not what most audiences of the day were expecting or used to. Divas 'died' frequently in musicals and operas, but usually with grace and finesse…not flailing around slathered in cow's blood. A silence descended over the onlookers, who had been reasonably enthusiastic thus far despite the ludicrousness of the operetta and the scathing reviews that had appeared in the press.

Having trodden the boards since the age of sixteen, Eulalia realised she was 'losing' the audience and guessed why. If they were revolted by gore and grue, well, she would try for pathos instead. Turning on the dramatics, she cast her plump arm across a furrowed brow and affected an expression of abject woe. Then, she slowly sank to her knees. "I am dying…" she sang in a low warble that sounded more like a gargle. "Dying…"

Someone in the crowd laughed.

Then someone else. A co-mingling of male and female laughter filled the auditorium.

Stunned, Isabella glanced over at Effie. Effie bit her lip. "There's been poor performances and empty houses aplenty in the last few weeks, but never outright laughter. Jesus, she'll go mad."

Eulalia tried to regain the crowd's attention one final time, lolling out over the edge of the stage, almost in the orchestra pit, her hair hanging over the edge, her heaving bosom on near-obscene display. One final operatic shriek of 'Dying…' tore from her mouth as she rolled over for one final dramatic death-spasm.

And then complete catastrophe struck. Eulalia's gown, too tight and adjusted a dozen times or more by the company's seamstresses, split down the back to reveal an ocean of frilly, diaphanous petticoats.

The Diva screamed and tried to sit up and cover her modesty. However, it was a futile struggle, her weight and her clothing pulling her down. One of the youthful violinists in the orchestra, following the frantic motions of the conductor, began to play his instrument in earnest in an attempt to cover her yowls of anguish…but in his eagerness, he swept his bow too high and caught the tip in Eulalia Fairbanks' coiffed hair. Or rather, in the styled wig she had worn to cover her own thin, greyish locks.

The wig was ripped from her head, flopping about on the tip of the bow like the skin of some slain animal. The poor musician, a young man fresh from music school, flushed crimson and in a motion born of his own terror and shock, waved his bow to release the frightful black clump clinging to it…sending the wig sailing into the nearby audience.

The house erupted into unbridled laughter. No comedy or variety show had ever received such applause. The lights suddenly came up, hissing and sizzling, revealing a sea of mirthful faces. One man in a top hat, clearly tipsy on wine tipped back during intermission, even fell out of his seat to roll on the frayed carpet.

Eulalia Fairbanks lumbered to her feet, huffing and puffing, trying to hold the back of her dress together with one hand. She looked out at the people laughing…laughing at HER, and then she fled the stage.

Hoots of derision followed her hasty departure. The backstage technicians panicked. The curtain came down with an almighty crash, knocking the unsuspecting dancers off their feet. Shrieking, they fell to the floor like skittles.

Isabella was thrown backwards, her spine meeting painfully with the ground.

"Are you hurt?" Effie was at her side, her face powdered with dust thrown up in the descending curtain's wake.

"My pride more than anything else." Isabella scrambled to her feet, marvelling again to see that flash of her unmarred leg, the white expanse that had once been marked by scars.

Effie clasped Isabella's hand. "No one's going out for curtain call after *that* disaster. Let's get dressed from here and back to the boarding house as soon as we can. Eulalia will blow up like a storm; you know it won't be pleasant to behold."

The two girls ran down the dank corridor leading to the dressing rooms. There were several large, decorated ones for the leads, full of mirrors with gilt frames lit by gas lamps, and plush chairs and stools lined with red velvet, and several communal ones for the swing and the extras—bare chambers with whitewashed walls that had turned yellow from smoke and age.

The lower-tier actresses had been assigned to one of the latter, which was shared by the wardrobe mistress and a young apprentice seamstress called Emily who mended the costumes, letting them out or drawing them in as appropriate, tidying up tears and replacing frayed lace and laces. Emily, a mousy girl with tortoise-shell rimmed spectacles resting on a pointed nose, was weeping violently as the actresses entered the room. She was being berated by the wardrobe mistress due to her 'failure' to see that 'Mistress Eulalia's costume fit correctly and the seams unlikely to burst.

"It wasn't my fault!" Emily wailed. Besides a fiercely pointed chin, she had sharp, protruding teeth, giving her a vaguely rat-like appearance. Dun-coloured hair flopped out of her bun as she rocked back and forth in despair. "Not my fault, Mistress Lola, if Madam Eulalia has got fat and won't admit it! I told 'er I wanted to give the dress a 'nip-tuck' but she was so angry, I thought she might 'it me!"

"Never, never speak of Eulalia Fairbanks' girth again—she might hear you!" The wardrobe mistress, Lola Bridges, heady in purple ruffles, with coiffed hair powdered to the same vibrant hue as her dress, glared at the younger woman in anger and dismay. "Stop making excuses and just apologise when she comes in. You'd better be good with a calming tongue, or you might soon be looking for another job, my girl!"

Isabella and Effie changed out of their costumes in haste while listening to this heated exchange. Emily was crying noisily now, afraid for her employment. "Don't sack me, Miss Lola, please. I wouldn't be able to pay my rent and I'd have nowhere to live. You know I'm plain as the day is long. I don't have no beau. I probably won't ever get married as I'm so homely, and I'd die before I went on the east end streets like other poor girls, frequenting the gin 'ouses..."

"Oh, girl, do shut up!" Lola put her hands on her ample hips and rolled her eyes in frustration. "As long as you heed my words, you shall remain in employment...but for goodness sake, do not rile the bloody Diva again!"

"We're off home now, Miss Lola." Effie handed their sweaty costumes to the wardrobe mistress to be cleaned and pressed. "What a night it has been. One I shan't want to remember."

"I am not surprised." Lips pursed peevishly, Lola Bridges draped the costumes over her arm. "I, for one, shall be glad when this show closes."

Isabella was fussing with a corset and with a dress that seemed all tiny eyeholes and laces. *You can do this*, she thought frantically. *Or rather, Arabella can...*

After what seemed an eternity, the two girls were ready to leave the theatre. Clad in prim hats and respectable day-gowns in muted colours, they hurried down the corridor leading to the stage door and the city streets beyond. They deduced that the door was open; cold night air swished along the passageway, stirring the hair they had scooped into neat buns.

"I see your admirer was in again," Effie said to Isabella. "I noticed him in the box."

Isabella nodded. "Does...does anyone have any idea who he is yet?"

Her friend looked thoughtful. "No. And I can imagine you must find it strange and disconcerting having him there night after night. But..." She gave a little smile, "he is young and, from a distance at least, looks exceedingly handsome. And he must have some wealth by his gifts and by his bearing."

"Handsome is as handsome does," Isabella said, rather primly. She thought it might sound like a Victorian type thing to say. "He looked hot" certainly would not do...

"Well, he's done nothing wrong, has he? Except not declare his intentions! He has sent you gifts, has he not?"

"Ah...yes, he has." Images appeared in her mind—the scarves, trinkets, bouquets...

"Then I think his intentions are perfectly clear," giggled Effie. "Maybe he is merely shy and there's nothing sinister here at all!"

Suddenly the sound of raised voices drifted down the corridor. One voice was higher-pitched than the other, needle-sharp, and incessant. And angry. Eulalia Fairbanks.

"Oh, blessed Jesus, what now?" said Effie.

The corridor bent to the left and coming around it, the girls could see the stage door and the doorman's admissions box, lit by a sputtering lantern on a hook.

Eulalia was blocking the exit whilst hanging onto the lapels of a tall man with bushy grey sideburns, who wore a jaunty top hat that almost touched the smoke-grimed ceiling. "You're not getting away so fast, George Huxtable!" she bellowed, her voice rumbling out like thunder. "I want compensation for tonight's humiliation!"

"Compensation!" Huxtable's own voice emerged, shrill and tremulous. "What compensation do you want, woman? It all went wrong tonight; it sometimes does!"

"You should never have coerced me into taking this ridiculous role, George! Fairies and fauns—fie on such silliness. I want high drama and superior operas and operettas where the audience will rise for me in a standing ovation!"

"That's never going to happen." The frustrated manager clasped Eulalia's wrists and tried to remove her hands from his jacket. "You are fortunate that I've found any work for you at all! Your time is over, Eulalia—face the truth! There are younger women on the stage these days, better looking, more talented and easier to work with!"

Eulalia screeched in wrath and bared her teeth like a beast, but at the same time, noticed Isabella and Effie standing huddled in the corridor, stunned by the unseemly commotion and too intimidated to try to push their way by.

"There...that girl..." She pointed at Isabella with a shaking hand. "That's the kind you're talking of, isn't it? A crude little street rat of no breeding or real talent. She tried to upstage me tonight; didn't you see? Or did you put her up to it, George?"

"Eulalia, do not be ridiculous. I hardly know the girl; she is mainly a chorus girl, a two-penny actress and dancer. Let her pass and stop shrieking like a fishwife—they'll hear you down to the Square with your immense projection!"

"I'm not letting that rancid little cow go anywhere." A crazy, out-of-control gleam filled Eulalia's eyes as if she had smoked some opium or taken some strange tincture while in her dressing room. "I want to know the truth; if she was put up to…to ruining me! Or perhaps she was just clumsy and inattentive—because she was more interested in that…that pigeon-livered ratbag who sits in the box every night, staring at her like some loon."

Effie flared in anger at the Diva. "That's not fair. He looks a perfectly respectable gentleman to me. More respectable than you…you great fat Whooperup! You make more noise than music these days, Eulalia Fairbanks, and everyone in town knows it! You are a laughingstock!"

Eulalia unleashed another titanic screech. Releasing George Huxtable's lapels, she launched herself at Effie and Isabella, cannoning into them like a maddened bull and knocking both girls into a heap on the floor. Her hand slashed down, striking off Isabella's hat and clutching a handful of her hair. "I'll teach you trollops to embarrass your betters," she slurred. "You're horrible hoydens, the pair of you."

"Let go of me!" cried Isabella, enraged. The pompous old bitch had assaulted her! Angrily, she grabbed Eulalia's wrists and pushed her back against the wall, hard.

Eulalia made a high-pitched sound that reminded Isabella of a passing freight train and lunged forward again, trying to slap Isabella's face. Effie was shouting and pounding on Eulalia's back.

As the women tousled and jostled in the hall, the angry Diva flung back her head and starting screaming for her personal bodyguards, as if she were the one being assaulted rather than the reverse.

Her personal minders, a group of thugs hired in the Docklands years ago when Eulalia's star was ascendant, came thundering down the corridor, eager for action—they saw little enough these days, for few admirers lingered by the stage door to gain an autograph from their mistress, let alone impede her progress to her carriage with declarations of desire. Most of the time the minders merely loitered outside her dressing room door drinking, gambling and playing cards, as they aged and grew fat, just like their employer.

One of them, a huge bald-headed oaf, descended upon the women. Foul breath blasted into Isabella's face as he reached out and lifted her by her collar, dangling her off the ground while he grinned and leered. "Can't have you getting a bit uppity, can we, missy? Look, you behave or I'll crush your legs and you'll never do nuffink again, no dancin' and nuffink else neither." He laughed lasciviously.

In response, Isabella bit his hand. He dropped her with a wild, surprised yell. "You little tart!" he howled. "I'll beat some humility into you…" His huge hand, speckled with spiky dark hair, curled into a menacing fist.

George Huxtable was waving his arms, his eyes bulging with fright. "Hubbard, no, this is utter madness! Harm the girl and the police will be all over us! We don't need that kind of bad publicity…"

"Shut yer gob, Huxtable!" growled Hubbard. "I've had my eye on this baggage for ages. Flitting about, acting better than she should. A bit 'o hard punishment should teach 'er 'er place." His grin stretched even wider, revealing missing front teeth and suppurating gums.

Suddenly a shadow fell over Hubbard, stretching long and black down the corridor. A man stood at the stage door, the moon through the open door an unblinking eye over his left shoulder.

"Unhand the lady," ordered a suave, well-mannered voice, but the tone was cold as ice. Cold enough to freeze the blood.

Unused to any challenge, Hubbard glanced up, his lip curling in an angry snarl. Isabella wriggled away from him, groping in the gloom for her fallen hat. Effie also struggled to her feet, pushing aside Eulalia Fairbanks with a thrust of a sharp elbow. The diva opened her mouth as if to release another outraged scream, but as she became aware of the newcomer, her jaw shut with an audible snap.

The stage doorman, a spidery figure with nicotine-stained hands and lips, hobbled from his box, holding up a candle-lantern. "We can't be having trouble 'ere!" he shrilled, an old man's vapid whine. He looked from Eulalia and Hubbard, to Isabella and Effie, to the stranger in the doorway "Fightin and pushin'. They might shut us down if the coppers get wind!"

"I will be only here a moment." The tall man turned in the stage doorman's direction and then back to the women in the hall.

Isabella gaped. It was her...no, *Arabella's*...admirer. The man who had watched her dance from the box, night after night. The giver of gifts. The nameless aristocrat whose purpose was unknown. A strange wave of both fear and elation passed through her.

"Miss, give me your hand and I will escort you away from this unseemly fracas..."

He put out his hand...and Eulalia Fairbanks' plump hand shot out to meet it. She sidled up to him, unaware that her wig, located in the stalls and hastily reattached in the dressing room, was hanging askew, or that her heavy eyeliner was so smudged she had taken on the appearance of a stout, overfed panda-bear. "How kind that you have taken an interest...but it is just a little misunderstanding," she said, her voice honeyed, soft, and no longer shrewish. "One of the chorus girls was playing up and being disrespectful."

"That's a lie!" Effie shot back, furious. Isabella dragged on her friend's arm, shushing her to silence. She still did not like the look of Hubbard, and there was no such thing as dialing 999 in this time.

Eulalia simpered at the man before her. He wore a long coat lined with red satin, decorated with golden buttons and braided trim. Dark hair in formal waves lay neatly against the nape of his neck and his face was white and sculpted, what one might describe as 'cruelly handsome', with a Grecian nose and sharp dent in the strong chin. Spicy, imported scent wafted from his person, and an ancient signet ring glimmered on his thumb. With his velvet hat and fashioned cane, he bore the air of an aristocrat, and Eulalia simply loved society's upper echelons. She imagined herself joining them…if she could find a wealthy man to marry.

"Did you enjoy the show?" she asked, seemingly having forgotten the disaster at the end of the performance. "Have you come to ask for my autograph? If you have purchased a programme, sir, I would be delighted to sign…" She snapped her fingers at the stage doorman, who, grumbling under his breath, put down his lantern and fumbled on his desk for a quill pen.

"Of course I have not come for an autograph." The tall man spoke, voice heavy with sarcasm. "What would I do with such a foolish thing? I have come to see Miss Arabella Lorne."

Eulalia's eyes bulged and a strangled sound came from deep within her throat. "Arabella! That minx! No, you cannot mean it…She is a trouble maker."

"I know exactly what I mean, Madam. Do not presume to tell me. Now…" he shook her clawing hand off roughly, "unhand me and step aside."

Mortally offended, Eulalia snatched her hand away with a black scowl. As the strange aristocratic man strode past her, she nodded meaningfully toward her thug Hubbard over the stranger's elbow.

Hubbard grinned. "Can't have our girls fraternisin' with men out of their class." He reached out and caught Isabella's wrist in a tight grip. "We look after ours, we do."

"Let go of me, you're hurting me!" cried Isabella. "And you're speaking nonsense. You are just Eulalia's bodyguard; you have no jurisdiction over the rest of us. You can't tell us what to do!"

The newcomer stopped in his tracks, gazing down at Hubbard—he was well over six feet tall—and Hubbard was short and squat by comparison. His eyes burned in the white, furious mask of his face.

"Let her go, cretin," he spat. "Or I will gut you right here!"

"Gut me! Will you now you bloody fop!" Hubbard pushed Isabella against the wall so hard her breath came out in a noisy rush, as he reached under his jacket and pulled out a nasty, curved little knife.

Effie began to scream when she saw the glint of metal; other women from the chorus joined in as they ran from their dressing rooms to see what the commotion was. Isabella slumped against the wall, hand to her mouth, horrified.

Lightning fast, the tall stranger lifted his jaunty cane. Flicking it with a deft motion of the wrist, a blade scythed out of the end. "I think mine is better," he said mockingly to Hubbard.

The Docklands thug gritted his teeth, hunching over as he assumed a menacing stance. He looked like a great, grunting, bald ape, rollicking from side to side in the corridor, his huge, boot-clad feet stomping on the cracked tiles below in some kind of shuffling war dance.

George Huxtable, sweat rolling down his lined brow, attempted to intervene in the fight. "This is most unacceptable!" he bellowed, waving his arms. "This is not a brawling yard! Take your battles away from here, and settle your differences like gentlemen. Or...or I shall send for the police. They have a station just at the other end of the Square you know!"

"Gentlemen!" The newcomer released a chilly laugh. "Only one of us here is a gentleman, I fear...but yes, I would rather settle this matter in a more civilised way, but settled it must be, for on behalf of the young lady, I want satisfaction. I would prefer pistols."

"Pistols!" Hubbard suddenly leered. "Sound all right t'me. I'm good with pistols, I am. I woz in the army once, long ago."

"Then why don't you both go and duel it out elsewhere!" said George Huxtable desperately. "This is not the place...not the place. A theatre, I ask you!"

"So, you will accept the challenge to a duel then, oaf?" asked the tall stranger, staring disdainfully at Hubbard.

"I will." Hubbard shoved his knife back under his coat.

"Then tomorrow it is, at dawn, in at Tothill fields. Be there before five...if you still dare, that is. As for the young ladies, let them pass unhindered. I do not know what iniquities take place within these walls, but whatever they maybe, the likes of you are not their master. This is not some harem in the palace of a foreign emir, sirrah. They are free to do as they will and clearly do not want to be in your company!"

Quickly and quietly, Isabella and Effie slipped behind their unexpected saviour's greatcoat and inched towards the door. Towards the night. Towards escape.

"I'll fight you...to the death, fop," mumbled Hubbard, expression murderous. "Tomorrow, just where ya stated. But tell me yer name, I wanna know what to tell 'em to carve on yer tombstone."

"My name is Stannion—Augustus Stannion. Sir Stannion. Yes, you remember that, remember that name."

The man, Sir Augustus, drew back his sword cane, retracting the blade, then began a retreat to the outside world, pushing the two young women before him.

"I will take you to your homes," he said, once they stood on the pavement outside the theatre, gesturing to a carriage that stood at the roadside under the lamp-lit boughs of a spreading beech tree. Encrusted with gold and silver, it clearly had once been a vehicle of high status, but now its flanks were scratched and scuffed, dull beneath the wan moonlight. Although it bore the hallmarks of one time great wealth, its condition also pointed to present hard times.

As Isabella gazed at Augustus Stannion, she decided her rescuer, her secret admirer, had a certain air of genteel poverty. Although he was certainly not as shabby as his battered carriage, his clothing showed signs of wear and was a poor fit. The styles looked somehow more old-fashioned than the other men she had seen—it was as if he had borrowed his father's garments. A faint smell came from the clothing, overriding his rich scent; not altogether unpleasant but chemical—one of the modern preservatives that kept clothes free of the depredations of moths when it was packed away.

Effie was speaking to Sir Augustus. "We are greatly appreciative of your assistance this night, Sir Stannion, but we would dare not trouble you for a ride to our...our humble abode. Isn't that right, Arabella?" She glanced at Isabella, brows raised.

Isabella jumped; she was halfway to the carriage, hand reaching for the silvered door handle. What had possessed her? It wasn't appropriate behaviour at all for a lady in this century. Even a lowly actress. And Augustus Stannion may have saved her from Hubbard but who knew what this strange man's own intentions actually were?

She drew back her hand, reluctantly. "Effie is right, sir. You have done enough for us. We could not impose. And...people might think it an impropriety. You surely know, sir, how young actresses are ofttimes the subjects of wicked rumours, especially if they are seen unchaperoned in the presence of patrons. I pray you understand. Our reputations are poor enough, as it is, with no provocation. We must take great care of our reputations." She hoped her speech would sound convincingly of the period.

"You are as decent and intelligent as you are fair." Augustus Stannion looked down at her from his great height. Isabella felt herself blush; no one had ever called her 'fair' before. Or rescued her from a knife-wielding thug. In fact, she'd never met anyone like Sir Augustus Stannion; her last boyfriend, more than two years ago, had been Brad, an estate agent whose main interested were football...and, well, football. She tried to concentrate on Stannion's words and not linger over his seeming attractiveness. "You must do as you see fit, Mistress Arabella. But I would ask you for a favour..."

"What is it?"

"Tomorrow I will proceed to my duel with that oaf who attacked you in the theatre."

"Otis Hubbard? Surely you will not..."

"He is beneath me, but I am a gentleman and keep my word in all things. It is my way. We will meet as planned at Tothill."

"But Hubbard will cheat, I am certain of it!" cried Isabella. "He will bring a posse of thugs and malcontents. You saw them. They may attack you. You need to call the police!"

"I have no doubt this Hubbard miscreant will try to chest; he is clearly a man without honour. And that is where you come in, Miss Arabella. I want you to be present as a witness to events. If anything untoward should befall me, I would beg you then race to my waiting carriage, fly to the nearest police station and give the names of the villains and the true course of events!"

"Why not just call the police first?" said Isabella. "They should be the ones to handle the situation."

Augustus looked at her strangely. "They can be summoned at need, yes. But my honour is more important. I want satisfaction. I do not wish to appear as a weakling. And I would like you to be my witness."

"But if Bella went with you, it would be so dangerous!" Effie breathed, butting in. "If you were hurt...or worse, sir, then those monsters would turn on Arabella...and then..." She swallowed, flushing.

Augustus Stannion ignored the girl's protest and fixed Isabella with a stern blue gaze. She felt a shiver inside, not altogether unpleasant. She should walk away, refuse, but.... "Arabella, you are fleet of foot, are you not? A dancer. Can you do this deed for me? I have chosen to fight not only for my honour...but for yours, remember." A low, almost pleading note entered the deep burr of his voice.

"But why?" The word tore from her trembling lips. "I'm...I'm no one..." *And I'm something you'd never expect...*

"my reasons are my own, and they sound mad to others' ears." He gave a brittle laugh. "Suffice it to say, I have only the most honourable intentions towards you, if you fear otherwise. The most honourable that can be. Tonight when I came to see your performance in that diabolical play alongside that huffing harridan, I had my best, and more special, gift for you yet. And a message to finally be delivered in person. Needless to say, my plans for a proper meeting went awry due to the unfortunate circumstances. However, you are here with me now and so we speak..."

Reaching into the breast pocket of his great coat, he brought out a trinket box carved from discoloured ivory. A coat of arms, worn away by many fingers, was painted on the lid. Snapping the box open, he revealed a ring nestled in a bed of frayed, pale blue silk. Fashioned from white gold, it was embedded with a crown of sapphires and diamonds. "This...my gift to you. It belonged to my deceased mother, Helena Stannion."

"For...for me?" Isabella stuttered, deep in shock. Effie's eyes were wide as saucers in her small, pert face. "I don't understand. Why would you give me a ring of such personal value? We...we've never even met before..."

"I know this whole scenario is unorthodox, Mistress Arabella. And I dare not explain it all to you lest you think me a lunatic. But... I want you to marry me. To come with me as my wife to my home, Elvingstone Manor."

Effie let out a small, startled squeak, like that of a mouse crushed in a trap. Her hand flew to her mouth in surprise.

Isabella merely stared at the ring in its box. Marry her! He must be joking, surely! "I...I cannot... I cannot think straight..."

Sir Augustus thrust the ring into her cold palm and forced her numbed fingers to close around it. "Whatever you decide, Mistress Arabella, the ring is yours to keep. My mother is long dead, and I will have no need of it if you refuse my suit. Now, I must away to my hotel on Regent Street. I pray you will attend me tomorrow at dawn for the duel. Farewell."

Turning swiftly on his heel, he leapt into the waiting carriage and signalled to a dark-cloaked driver wearing an immense top hat. The two bay horses whinnied and pawed, then clattered off down the city streets, hooves drawing sparks from the night-dewed pavement.

"Jesus, Arabella, I think the world has gone mad!" cried Effie, watching them depart. "Let's go before something else uncanny happens!"

"Lead on," said Isabella, not trusting the constant fading and receding of Arabella's memories.

Holding hands, the two young women raced down the street, past teeming crowds newly disgorged from theatres, taverns, coffeehouses and restaurants. Old women staggered from gin halls, drunk and toothless, cackling like storybook witches; burly men in hats with brims that hid their eyes whistled and hooted at any female under sixty. Down on the embankment by the Thames, a lone fiddler stood on the base of the statue of some former prime minister and played a haunting air as the mist rolled in off the turgid, foul-smelling water.

Isabella and Effie ploughed through the crowds, cutting across several small squares where fountains gushed into mossy basins and lovers walked, secrecy ensured by the descending shadows. A female vagrant in a soiled dress was washing a ragged under-slip in one fountain while singing softly to herself; she glanced up nervously as the young actresses swept by—she was missing one eye.

Passing down towards the wharfs, the girls came to the boarding house where they resided—a squat, old building that had once been a small, private hospital. Dark yellow brick, tiny windows with bars, a roof of red tiles. It had a green wooden porch guarding an oak door strong enough to withstand a battering ram, which was lit by a dinted lantern dangling on a hook. Moths skittered around the lantern, bashing off the glass as they attempted to immolate themselves in the oily flame.

Effie fumbled in her bag and brought out a rusty key. She thrust it into the lock and the door opened with a clunk, allowing the two girls to tumble into the hallway.

The passage was low and dark, with a threadbare carpet faded to non-descript brown. High walls were the yellow of old vomit, and a single, sighing lamp cast greenish shadows that swayed and swelled. Rows of unpainted doors ran down the corridor toward a barred window that looked out over the roof and a slumped, precarious chimneystack—unused, for a large bird was nesting atop it.

"Shush, we must be quiet." Effie pressed a finger to her lips. "We don't want Missus Gold coming out and giving us hell."

"No," said Isabella. "We don't." *I have had enough fighting with strange women…*

"We're a bit late on rent," said Effie, "and you know what a miser old Goldie is. She keeps every penny of the rent money stored under her bed, guarded by that smelly Bulldog of hers—Brutus."

Effie pointed to a peeling notice nailed to the wall. "Just 'cause she had a hard life and lost her man young, she tries to make others' equally hard so she tries to rule her house with an iron hand— Look! *'No pipe smoking, drinking, music, loud laughter, immodest garb, profanity, or visitors of the opposite sex. Any infraction will result in immediate expulsion'*—and to add insult to injury, she keeps the goods of those she evicts!"

"Surely that is illegal! Theft!" Isabella was horrified.

Effie shrugged. "Her place, her rules, right or wrong. We'll need to be careful. She'll be awake, as she always is. I swear she presses her ear to the door just to hear if anyone should stub their toe and utter a curse word."

The girls tiptoed down the hall, grimacing at every creak of the floorboards, heading for the room at the end near the barred window. As the key clicked in the lock, another door in the hall opened with a squeal and a bony female face peered out, suspicious and more than a bit malevolent. "There she is! Hurry!" hissed Effie in fright, and she pushed Isabella into the room beyond, shutting the door firmly behind them both.

The rented room was shabby and dismal, with a tiny window giving views across the roof of some derelict tenements. It had a small fireplace, dusty with ash, its ornamental surround made of cracked blue tiles. Two narrow beds stood in either corner, and there was an ancient black stove and a rickety chair. An earthenware chamber pot stood under the window ledge, as far away from the living space as possible. Isabella stared at it in dismay. The bed sheets looked dirty and she was sure she'd catch 'passengers' from them. And to pee in a pot, without even a curtain around her!

"I'll put the kettle on." Effie approached the stove. "Need a cuppa after all that palaver tonight!"

Isabella flopped onto the edge of a bed; springs creaked and groaned under her weight. Reaching into her purse, she drew out the ring Augustus Stannion had given her and stared at it. His offer, his crazy offer of marriage...if she was stuck in this Victorian-type world, stuck in a dream, taking his offer might be better than staying here. Of course, she would try to convince him she was not marriage material later on; she might be caught out of time, but she was no man's pawn, bought by a stranger offering a glittery ring. That was sick...

Yet...she could not stop thinking of Augustus's steely blue eyes and stern jaw, and almost without thinking, she slipped it on her wedding finger. The band felt cold as ice. It fit surprisingly well, as if it were made for her...

"Are you going to go?" Effie passed a cracked china teacup to her companion on a mismatched saucer.

"Go where?"

"To witness the duel, as he asked."

"No...well, I don't know!" Isabella's eyes widened and she pulled Augustus' ring from her finger—though she did not put it away but stared into its glittering heart. "The danger...the strangeness of it all..."

"You know what I'd do?" said Effie coyly, twisting a strand of her blond curls.

"You tell me."

"I'd go. And marry 'im. That's what 'e said 'e wants. What more do you want?"

Isabella bit her lip. How could she explain that her sensibilities were modern ones, and that women did not go around feeling overjoyed to receive marriage proposals from strangers? "It's is ridiculous. He couldn't possibly have meant it."

"You have his ring…" Effie nodded toward Isabella's hand.

"Yes, yes, I do. I will need to give it back…"

"You are going then…"

Arabella fell silent, toying with the ring. Diamonds and sapphires flashed and flared.

"What 'ave you got to lose, Bella? What? We won't be going back to the theatre after what happened tonight, you know that, don't you? That old cow Eulalia will never permit it. We've been sacked, you can be sure of it. We'll need to find new jobs, once the ruckus dies down…and that might take a while. We're going to have to leave Gold's rooming house…once we get our final pay, if we ever do. We won't be able to pay the rent."

"What have I to lose? Well…" Isabella slipped the ring back on her finger again. In her case, nothing. She did not know how she came here, how to get back, how a 21st century photographer came to inhabit the body of a 19th century girl. Arabella might have some relatives about, but she intuited the girl had no close family; like so many in a pre-antibiotic world, they had died from infection and flu. But still, the whole idea of *marrying* this man made her stomach lurch with queasy fear. She was not and never had been some fool living in a fantasy dream of romance with a rich man…she'd heard the lurid tales of naïve girls who had gone off with seemingly decent men and ended up floating in the river. In both the present century and the one almost two hundred years in the future.

"I am going to go to my Uncle Will's," said Effie. "He has a cottage in Surrey. He's my only kin; I think she'd be happier with me living with her than treading the boards, if I'm honest. He believes all actresses are all immoral. He'll probably push me towards one of the local lads…I remember Billy Bates liked me."

"Would you be happy with that?" asked Isabella, still toying with Stannion's ring. "You've trained for your career so long and hard. You have a beautiful singing voice"

"And got nowhere with it. As for being happy, I suppose I could be," said Effie thoughtfully, sipping at her tea. "Maybe I've finally got performing out of my blood. You know…I'm tired of livin' hand to mouth, starving myself to fit my costumes, and dancin' till my legs feel bruised." She rubbed her shins, expression one of pain. "I just want to settle and have my own brood now. Funny, two years ago I'd never have admitted such a thing. What about you, Bella; what is it you truly want?"

"I don't know, Effie—I truly don't." Isabella let out a deep sigh, her shoulders slumping. *To go home, to my rotten, overpriced flat and my credit card debts and my nights in front of the television…or peering endlessly down a camera lens…*

"Then you should go to the duel tomorrow. Go see Augustus Stannion fight for your honour and his. And if he still wants to wed you when all is said and done—do it."

"What if Hubbard, God forbid, should win and I'm left there alone?"

"Then use this…" Effie reached down to her laced-up boot and pulled out a narrow knife. She handed it carefully to Isabella. "I've always kept this on me for protection. Won't need it if I go back to Uncle John's. You might, though. A parting present for you"

Isabella gazed at the gleaming knife, staring at her troubled face reflected upon the blade

Then she reached out and took it.

She was going to the duel tomorrow.

Shivering, she woke before dawn. Grey light spilt through tattered curtains onto bare floorboards. Rising from her bed, she pulled on a plain, workaday dress and then bundled all the rest of Arabella's threadbare garments into a large cloth bag. Augustus' ring was still on her finger; she had left it on all night. On the other side of the room, Effie was still sleeping, her breath noisy between slightly parted lips.

Isabella thought about waking her to say goodbye but decided against it. She looked so peaceful, and besides, Isabella hated farewells. "Good luck, Effie," she murmured instead of goodbye. "Hope you find your Mister Right and that simple cottage one day soon!"

Leaving the room, she crept silently down the hall and away into the cold morning. The streets were still and silent, except for the occasional yowling of a stray cat. Heels clicking on the pavement, Isabella hurried between the towering tenements and made her way towards the river.

She knew roughly where she was heading, despite a plethora of unfamiliar buildings. Tothill, the old duelling ground, was near the palace of Westminster…which fire had partly destroyed only recently. She was not able to use Big Ben as a marker, however—it was some years before it would be built… Tothill was also the site of the notorious Bridewell prison, where forced labour for the so-called indolent took place…although if she remembered rightly, the prison had closed now, and was moved to a location nearer to Vauxhall. In the future, Westminster Cathedral would take over much of the fields but that was more than fifty years ahead…

As the sun began to rise, its rim bursting through a low bank of clouds, she reached Tothill fields. In the distance were the ragged. fire-blackened ruins of the great medieval palace of Westminster. Isabella stared at it for a moment, taking in what no one of her generation had ever seen. Then with a sigh, she hurried toward the waste ground, where unsavoury deals were finalised and illegal battles fought with sword and pistol.

Crossing a narrow brick bridge that forded a weed-clogged artery of the Thames, Isabella entered the fields. Warily, she glanced around. The Toot Hill, an artificial hill built in some remote, unknown age—locals spoke of Elves and fairies, of strange dancing lights at the full moon—thrust up from the middle of the greenery, its rounded head wreathed by a swirling band of grey mist. Near to it, stood the ruins of a red brick building bonded into earlier yellow sandstone. What it had once been, Isabella had no clue— maybe something to do with Bridewell prison? It was unrecognisable as anything now—its walls swathed in ivy, the interior filled with long, tangling weeds that whispered in the wind.

A sudden noise from behind made Isabella leap in alarm. Glancing hastily over her shoulder, she saw the dim outlines of figures half-hidden in the mist as they trudged towards the bridge. A loud, coarse voice, made strangely inhuman by the thick vapours, was bawling, "I bet 'e don't turn up, the fancy ponce! Bet he turns yellow on us."

Isabella subdued an instinctive gasp of fear. Hubbard and his cronies were here early! Fearful, she ran into the old ruin, pressing herself against the ivy-cocooned inner wall. The mist swirled in, cold and clammy off the great river, reeking of green things, dead things, stagnation and mire. She hoped it would form an ample cloak of invisibility that would shield her from hostile eyes.

Footsteps sounded nearby, heavy thuds on the wet grass. Peering through a broken doorway, Isabella spied a lantern bobbing in the fog. "Blast this mist! She recognised Hubbard's harsh voice. "Can't see a goddamned thing! If it doesn't lift, there may not be a fight."

"May not be one anyway," sniggered one of his unseen companions.

"No, that's true. Mebbe for the best. I may be a decent enough marksman but it's been a few years since I was in the army."

"And was dishonourably discharged…" said the other, laughing.

"Yeah, I was. Lucky to escape gaol, but I managed to convince 'em she led me on… Anyroad, I am taking no chances… When Mr Fancypants shows up—if he does—it'll be one pace, two paces and then before the third is over…BANG!"

"You big cheat, Otis!" laughed the thug's unseen companion.

"Only way to get by, me mate. Only way in this bloody bastard of a world. Cheat the stupid, beat the rest. Now, where the hell is that blasted fop?"

Hiding amid the greenery, Isabella pressed her hand over her mouth. Hubbard intended to kill Augustus Stannion by treachery, just as she'd thought he might! Fear seized her and she longed to race out of the field, but if Hubbard spotted her….

The thug moved on with his party of scoundrels and she breathed a sigh of relief. Peering through a ruinous arch, she saw Hubbard head over to a stand of lean birch trees, their thin boles swaying in the chill dawn wind. Slumping onto a tree stump, he took a swig from a bottle, which he then passed to his friends.

A few minutes later, hooves rattling on gravel dragged her attention away from the villain. Back on the red brick bridge, a carriage loomed through the dissipating fog. A faded coat of arms gleamed on the doors. "It's Augustus!" she breathed, not certain if she felt relieved or even more apprehensive.

For a moment, fear warred with courage and with common sense. Then, heedless Hubbard and his minions, she sprang from hiding and ran pell-mell towards the carriage as it rocked over the hump of the rickety bridge.

Waving her arms, she rushed out in front of the horses, uncaring of her own safety. The driver uttered an oath and drew sharply on the reins. The carriage slowed to a near-stop and the side-door flew open. Augustus Stannion's pale, stern, face appeared as he leant from the door, hand gripping the gilt handle.

"Christ, girl!" he snapped. "What were you thinking of, running out like that? You could have been killed!"

"I did it to help you!" she shot back, a frisson of anger running through her. "You needn't be so rude! I have overheard something you need to know—it may save your life!"

"I understand your concern but I need no help, Mistress Arabella. I can take care of myself. Although I dare say, I am glad you are here. And…your concern is most touching." He looked her up and down with approval…and yet his eyes stayed strangely cool, dark. It was not a look of love, or even desire.

"You don't know what I have to say!" she cried, annoyed and uncomfortable under that inscrutable gaze.

"Speak on then, Miss Lorne. I am guessing you have news about the plans of our dear friend Hubbard. That you've heard whispers he will try to cheat and take me unawares."

Isabella stared. "Yes. Exactly."

"I suspected as much. I am no one's fool. Now jump into the carriage before attention is drawn to you."

His long, graceful hand, white-gloved, stretched towards her. She reached out and clasped it; strong fingers, taut as wire wound with hers. Embarrassed, she stumbled clumsily into the carriage and slumped on the padded seat next to him.

"Hubbard said he would fire before the final call was given."

"That is no surprise." The corner of Augustus' mouth lifted; Isabella noticed his hand had now drifted down to touch the barrel of a fine pistol lodged in a holster at his waist. "That is one of the favoured ploys of a treacherous cheat."

"What are you going to do? Confront him? Refuse to fight knowing he's a cheater?"

"Do not be foolish, Miss Arabella. Honour, and so much more, is at stake here. The duel will take place, threats of dishonesty or no."

"But he will attempt to kill you!"

"Yes, but knowing what his feeble plan is, I am more than ready. He will fire before the count of three, and I will fire before he does."

"But…but surely that makes you…"

He laughed, his voice hard. "What? As dishonourable as he? Maybe it does, madam. But a proper duel is between gentlemen. Hubbard is no gentleman—pah, such scum as he scarcely merits the term human! I am not bound to any rules duelling against the likes of Otis Hubbard."

The carriage rolled on through the fog for a few yards, halting in the lee of the decayed building on Toothill fields. Augustus Stannion stuck his head out the window and glanced around.

"Hubbard!" he shouted, his voice partly muffled by the fog. "I can see your lantern. Are you ready to duel? Let us get this matter over. I have business to attend to later in the day." Opening the carriage door, Stannion stepped out into the mist. Isabella climbed warily after him, peering over his shoulder.

Hubbard and his men leapt to their feet and marched forward from the stand of fog-cloaked trees. "You got your coffin makers ready, toff?" growled Hubbard, with a leer. "Well, well, well, I see you got the slattern with you too! Looking forward to getting to know her better, once you're cold on the ground. Much better." He grabbed the crotch of his baggy trousers in an obscene fashion.

"The lady you dare speak of is to be my wife," said Augustus icily, and Isabella jumped at the sound of those unbelievable words. Again, she was struck by the madness, the unreality of the situation—from a normal life in 21st century London, to becoming an actress in Victorian times, who had a secret admirer, about to embark on a duel to the death. A small piteous moan escaped her lips, and she fingered the little knife Effie had given her. She'd need to use that if Augustus should lose the fight...

"Yer wife, eh? So that's what they are callin' whores these days," leered Hubbard, reaching to his belt and pulling out his pistol. He played around with the gun, twirling it like some child's toy—a dirty, brutal-looking thing, much dinted, with a barrel of dark, worn metal.

Augustus did not rise to the bait; his features remained impassive. Pulling out his own pistol, he examined it thoroughly while saying to his coachman, "By Christ, this Hubbard is an ugly fellow. If he takes a wound in the face, it will not make much difference...but it would be a shame if such an oaf should ruin the Stannion profile. Shall I ask that he shoot no higher than my chest?"

Overhearing his words, Hubbard's cronies began to snigger and nudge each other. Otis Hubbard scowled, his brow lowering to primitive levels. "None of your bloody clever lip, fop! Let's get on with it. If it gets too late and we're spotted, the coppers will be down on us like wolves!"

"Very well," said Augustus brusquely. "I am already tired of such lowly company." He leant over to Isabella, speaking out the side of his mouth. "Get back into the carriage and make no outcry or motion that may divert my attention during the duel. If anything goes wrong, my man will drive you out of here without delay. It would not be safe to deposit you anywhere in the city; I've given instructions to take you to my aunt Allegra's mansion in Kent. She is always eager for good domestics; I know that it is not the employment a young performer would wish for, but you would be safe with her and your safety is the main thing."

Isabella swallowed nervously but nodded her acquiescence and climbed back into the carriage.

Augustus walked over to Hubbard; they were of similar heights but Hubbard was twice as wide, an ogre of a man bloated from drink and overeating. "Are you prepared?"

"Ready as I'll ever be, fop!"

"Good. Back to back then... three paces, then fire. I would prefer my man to call, if you don't mind." He gestured to a smaller, hatted man who was seated beside the coachman.

"Nah, I want mine to call," argued Hubbard. "Don't trust you."

"And I should trust you, guttersnipe? But very well, as you wish."

One of Hubbard's gang ambled forward; a shock-haired youth with a split lip and a golden ring in his ear. "I'm Roger Thrubwell, I'll do it—I got a loud enuff voice."

Pistols in hand, the two combatants stood back to back. Stannion towered over his opponent, but Hubbard was twice as wide with muscles popping beneath a veneer of fat. "So," bawled Thrubwell. "It will be three long paces. One, two, three. Then I yell 'fire.' Got it?"

"Got it," retorted Augustus, his tone filled with sarcasm.

"Then let's see what Fate holds in store an' fer whom," said Roger Thrubwell with a tombstone grin. "Ready? One...."

The opponents took a great, long stride away from each other, facing in opposite directions. Their pistols gleamed in their hands, dull in the early morning greyness.

"Two!" roared Thrubwell. One of his colleagues began to beat on a dirty old drum, tapping out a funereal rhythm. The duellists took another long stride away from each other.

Sitting in the confines of the carriage, Isabella began to shiver uncontrollably. Teeth gritted, chilled hands knotted together, she began to pray. She was not a religious person, but her mind chuntered on *Ohgodohgodohgod...* Outside, the horses, unnerved by Thrubwell's strident shouts or perhaps sensing the tension in the air, began to prance and fret, setting their harnesses jingling. The coachmen seized the reigns, seeking to keep them under control.

"And thr..."

Swift as a striking serpent, Augustus Stannion whipped around, standing sideways to his enemy, so that he gazed straight over his right shoulder at Otis Hubbard. His right leg shielded his left; his stomach, washboard flat anyway, was tightly drawn in. His gloved hand moved, and the sound of his pistol firing tore into the misty morning.

Hubbard turned nearly as quickly as his enemy, his pistol firing mere seconds after Stannion's. However, his broad frame faced his opponent head on, wide and solid as a mountain. Augustus Stannion's bullet took him in the thigh, while his shot whizzed past the torso of the slimmer combatant.

Hubbard roared in agony and fell to one knee. Blood spurted from his wound and created red dew upon the ground. Nonetheless, he grappled with his pistol, preparing to take another shot.

Cool and composed, Augustus fired again while Hubbard's finger was still on the trigger. This time, the bullet entered Hubbard's broad chest and felled him. The impact flung him backwards, arms flailing, and then he collapsed in a massive, bloodied heap, his eyes staring sightlessly up at the lightening sky.

His cronies fled, skittering out of Tothill fields like frightened rats.

Augustus Stannion approached the fallen body of his foe. "No priest needs to be called. He is beyond that. I dare say no priest could have helped him anyway, and no doubt, he is already burning in Hell."

Isabella leant out of the carriage, still trying to control the shaking that had gripped her. "What shall we do with his body?" Surely, they couldn't just leave Hubbard there, criminal or no?

"Leave him. If his monstrous friends do not return for him, others will show up to make use of his grotesque corpse. Those who sell body parts for study, for instance. In death, he might do some good aiding the practitioners of science."

"I feel faint," whispered Isabella. She'd never seen someone killed before. "I did not realise…there would be so much blood…"

"I know women are prone to vapours—there constitutions are weak—but remember well what he would have done to me…and what even worse things he would have done to you." Augustus knelt beside his slain opponent and began unbuttoning the blood-soaked shirt with clear distaste.

"What are you doing?" Isabella gazed on with horror, her gorge rising. "Surely you are not going to strip him?"

"No, I am just taking a little…memento." Taking a small crystal phial from his pocket, he filled it with Otis Hubbard's blood.

Isabella gasped in horror. "Why on earth are you taking his blood?"

"It's nothing you need to know about," said Augustus coldly, thrusting the full phial inside his greatcoat. "Let us just say—a tribute. You will learn in time. Now, get in the carriage and sit back down. We must leave this place as soon as we might. We do not want to be hindered by uncomfortable questions in a police inquiry! After all, my dearest Arabella, we have a wedding to prepare for!"

"Are you truly going to marry me?" Isabella glanced at Augustus Stannion as his carriage careered over potholes in the long country road. Fields and hills flashed by, and villages with pretty, timber-framed houses and churches bearing tall, darning-needle church spires.

"So you doubt that I am a man of my word? I have said so, more than once. We will be married."

"But…it is…unorthodox." *More than you know, Augustus…* "You know me only from my stage appearances."

"That does not matter. My mind is made up. I have my reasons."

"Perhaps I am entitled to know them." Gathering courage, Isabella sat bolt upright on her seat. "I am not some possession, some slave to be bought, even with a pretty ring on offer. Slavery has been outlawed since 1833, or have you forgotten, Sir Augustus?" She suppressed a smug smirk; he youthful, hated history lesson had come in handy at last.

Eyebrows raised, Augustus stared at Isabella then began to laugh. "You have spirit…I did wonder if that should prove the case. Yes, you have a right to know more that I've told you, clearly. This marriage is merely a contract, not a love-match, and I wish to make it for reasons personal to me. One day I might tell you the full story…or I might not, as the mood takes me."

"A strange way to begin a marriage."

"For some, but such marriages have existed since time immemorial. Just let it be known, Miss Arabella, that upon my word as a knight and a gentleman, I will not abuse you with words or with my hand. Although my family is now an impoverished one, alas, you will still live in a grand manor, with as many trappings of finery as I can still afford. I am sure this will be far more pleasant than what you would expect as a jobbing chorus girl."

Isabella's ears burned. "You don't have to insult my job. Far better than being a seamstress, locked in some sweathouse, or a dull secretary shuffling papers."

Again, Augustus smiled but it was a thin smile. "I speak but the truth, harsh though it may seem. You may find other things I…require strange, too. Although I seek a wife to give me a veneer of respectability." he laughed as if at a private joke, "there is more to it. Do not expect soirées in the city or fancy trips abroad. I despise them, cannot afford them. Indeed, don't expect many visitors to the manor; I have but few friends. Once a month you may shop in the local town, maybe once a year we will go to London, to visit the theatre and be seen in society."

Isabella's brow furrowed; she didn't like the sound of these 'terms' at all, although she felt relieved that Augustus wanted a wife in name only. "You will hold me there almost like a prisoner. Which brings me back to my earlier point about slavery. You may not abuse me but I will be your possession."

"Even if our marriage was of the more regular sort, many men would see you as such," said Sir Augustus in a clipped tone. Suddenly he thrust his hand out the window and waved to the coachman, who reined in the horses, pulling them in beside a roadside ditch.

Augustus shoved the carriage door open; beyond, sunlight gleamed on green fields, making them glow with golden warmth. Clouds were billowing over the head of a rounded hill topped by birches with fluttering leaves. A long path wound through the growing corn to a little hamlet with thatched houses and a duck pond on the green. "If my proposal is truly odious to you, Miss Arabella, you are free to go and we will never meet again on God's green earth. Make your decision swiftly, for I would be at Elvingstone Manor by dusk and the miles ahead are still many."

Isabella made a movement toward the carriage door and the freedom beyond. She could smell warm, damp soil and hear birds singing in the trees and bushes. Part of her longed to be away from the unnerving man at her side, but the other half of her...*What on earth was wrong with her?*

"I may have no other opportunity like this one." The words slid thickly from her tongue, and, dazed, she slammed the carriage door shut and fell back into her seat. With no place to go, there really was no choice.

"Good; you've seen sense." The secret, slightly cruel smile flashed again. "Then we will speak no more about it."

The carriage rolled on. The blue of the sky faded to warm, burnished bronze as the dying sun lit up scudding clouds. In the distance clustered a row of black shapes—tall townhouses and a smattering of church spires, one of which was crooked, bent at an odd angle. "The town of Chesterfield," said Sir Augustus. "Where they say the church spire has doubled back to gaze in shock at the last virgin bride to step over the threshold." He laughed harshly.

"Yes, I've heard that bit of folklore," said Isabella quietly. *And I've seen that warped spire, where the medieval carpenters used wood that was too green, when passing in my car on the A61. Bet that would shock you, Master Stannion!*

"Chesterfield is the nearest town to Elvingstone Manor, my dear. Soon we shall be home."

The carriage turned sharply at a crossroads where a gallows stood, empty noose dangling in the wind. The obscene wooden tree bore no fruit but the sinister, long shadow it cast made Isabella shudder.

"Whatever is the matter?" asked Augustus, noticing.

"The gallows...I've never seen one up close. Do they have many of them up here?"

"Oh yes, this is quite a lawless region, near to wild moorland, the Peaks and dense forest, hence one of the reasons I want you kept safe behind Elvingstone's walls," Augustus retorted but there was a dark twinkle in his eyes.

"You tease me again."

"I do. No, you are not in any danger, not from wicked men at least. At one time brigands would rampage down from Peakland to Sherwood and do High

Toby upon the road. No man's money nor his wife and daughters were safe. But the King's Justice has put an end to that in the last few decades, and now the Queen in his place…the gallows remain, however, as a reminder to all miscreants. You will find, Arabella…" he leant close to Isabella, engulfing her in his shadow, "that in this shire, the past is never very far away. Never far at all. We learn to *respect* it, if not love it."

A few more miles passed. Trees began to appear on either side of the road—stands of oak, ash and elder. "That woodland is called Druid's Grove," said Augustus. "It was planted by the Normans as part of a royal forest, or so the legends go. There was a hunting lodge on the present site of Elvingstone Manor. We are not far away now."

The carriage swung off the rutted road and began making its way down a drive that wound into the distance like a coiling serpent. At the end of it was a huge, wrought-iron gate, black metal with gold-painted scroll and sunburst, and, painted in colour, the Stannion family crest. Just above it, loomed a shield bearing the Royal Arms of England. "A gift from old King Charles many years ago," explained Augustus. "My family were supporters in his time of need."

The driver leapt from the carriage and opened the gates. They swung back, allowing the carriage to pass through unimpeded. Isabella stared out the window in fascination. On either side were woodlands filled with Rhododendron bushes and blue hydrangeas. Carefully pruned topiary rose like fantastical children's tops, and winding woodland walks were lined with twisted stones reminiscent of ruined Druidical altars. Just beyond, a sullen lake, unstirred by any wind, stretched out between the trees. A fountain stood in the middle—two nymphs supporting a circle of rough-hewn rock—but no water jetted into the sky.

"Why is the fountain not running?" asked Isabella, then wished she had not. Perhaps, it was impertinent to ask.

"Blocked," said Augustus shortly. "You will find many things at the manor have not been kept up in the fashion I would like. Such is one's fate when one's father gambled profusely and then drank the family fortune away."

Up in the far distance, Isabella could now see the shape of a house, long and low, with wings stretching out from the main front. The roofline was castellated, the jagged row of crenellations biting at the dimming sky.

Isabella had expected to be overawed by opulence, but instead, a slight shiver ran down her spine. The house looked gloomy and unwelcoming.

The carriage crunched over gravel and pulled up at the main door of the manor house. A few servants waited, standing to attention like a King's guards. Most were old, poker-faced, dressed in uniforms of yesteryear that seemed dreadfully prim and old-fashioned. Patching was visible on skirts and hems, collars bore a tint of grey, as if they had been washed too many times.

Augustus handed Isabella down from the carriage. "Your new home, Elvingstone Manor," he said, and she suspected it was not pride in his voice but sarcasm.

Isabella glanced up at the façade of the house. It was a strange building indeed, one side wrought of dull, yellowish stone with rows of square windows blocked by heavy, dark shutters, while on the other side, the masonry was interspersed with crumbling red brick. A single bay window with old, deep-hued, mullioned glass sagged out of the brickwork, looking as if it might tear away altogether in a strong wind and crash in ruins to the ground below.

"How strange," whispered Isabella. "They don't match. The two sides of the house, I mean."

"No, they don't," said Augustus. "Remember how I said a hunting lodge stood on the site first? The window is the last remnant bar a fragment of wall and some beams in the smoking room and kitchen. When my grandfather knocked down the old lodge, which was in terrible repair, he decided to keep the few sound elements for posterity. The glass in the window is three or four hundred years old. It has seen the births and deaths of many generations of Stannions."

He turned to the door and the waiting servants, still frosty-faced and still as standing stones. "This is Carver, our butler, Cook Tumnel, Jock the stable master, and Jemima the head maid, plus our other domestics Pearl, Alice and Sairey. You'll be in the care of Nanny Burtoncappe—she was my nanny as a child. She's very old and frail, hence she awaits inside, out of the chill wind. She will help you prepare for the wedding. She is very loyal...and understanding. And when her mind is sound, a font of knowledge."

Carver the Butler was opening the manor's door, a huge slab of oak painted black and bearing a brass knocker of a lion's head. "You first, Mistress Arabella," said Augustus Stannion, with a slight bow.

Isabella stepped into the hall of Elvingstone. Stopped. Tried not to gasp. It was like something from a twisted faery tale, a lurid fantasy...but not a bright one, where the princess triumphs after the ball. Instead, it was reminiscent of a dark fantasy where apples are poisoned and wicked women rolled to their deaths in barrels filled with spikes.

The hall was gloomy, lit only by fizzling gas lamps. Gold fan vaulting soared overhead, while on the walls hung damp-splotched red velvet wallpaper. All along the hall were mirrors that rose floor to ceiling, and between them in niches were upholstered thrones, empty save for dust. It looked as if hardly anyone had cleaned the mirrors and chairs for years; dust motes drifted upwards, disturbed by Isabella's passage, pale ghosts in the fading light, reflected a dozen times in the mirrors.

Augustus did not seem to notice his bride-to-be's hesitance. He grasped her arm. "Over here, my dear. The drawing room." He ushered her into another room behind two large, sliding oak doors.

The drawing room continued with the mock-ancient décor of the hall of mirrors. Again, gold vaulting leapt above, only now the walls were covered emerald green fabric wallpaper. A huge fireplace carved with roses disgorged old ash into a blackened brazier, while on wooden panels above the mantel painted jesters cavorted in bell-tipped caps. Heraldic shields and stylised faces of English Kings and Queens gazed down from niches.

"Who…who did all this?" Isabella let her eyes wander over the faces, the gurning jesters, the frowning Kings and smiling Queens in their dalmatic robes.

"My grandfather began it. He was an antiquarian and loved the medieval past. My father continued his work…mostly when he was drunk. I carried on, too, when I was bored. I must admit I am quite a fan of the…ancient, the gothic. There is more a similar vein, in other rooms throughout the manor and in the grounds, but it is far too dark to show you now. I am sure you must be weary after all that has occurred. I will introduce you to Nanny Burtoncappe."

Augustus led Isabella away from the hall and up a set of creaking stairs that wound through the heart of the house. At the top, corridors stretched away into the gloom, darker and plainer than those below. Dusty paintings of ancient Stannion ancestors gazed solemnly from gilt frames. Some of the doors to the rooms hung ajar; Isabella uttered a little, audible gasp as she saw a cradle in one, swathed in a filthy white sheet.

Augustus suddenly went white and kicked that particular door shut. Booms reverberated through the house. "You'll find lots of old rubbish in Elvingstone," he said in a glacial tone.

At the end of the corridor was a bedroom with a four-poster bed. The scent of tallow and lavender drifted out. A dwarfish figure wrapped in a long shawl was sitting on a seat beside the bed, rocking back and forth while singing in a cracked tone, "*Said my lord to his ladye,*

> *as he mounted his horse,*
> *Take care of Lord Lankyn,*
> *who lies in the moss. (*
> *Said my lord to his ladye,*
> *as he rode away,*
> *Take care of Lord Lankyn,*
> *who lies in the clay.*
> *Let the doors be all bolted,*
> *and the windows all pinned,*
> *And leave not a hole*
> *for a mouse to creep in.*
> *The doors were all bolted,*
> *and the windows were pinned,*
> *All but one little window,*
> *where Lord Lankyn crept in."*

"What is this?" cried Isabella in horror, listening to the ominous words.

"It is but an old woman's fancy," said Augustus dismissively. "Humour Nanny, I bid you; she has always been good to me. Now I must be off to make some preparations of my own. The vicar will be at the church by noon on the morrow. I will send for you. You must not be late."

He stalked away, leaving Isabella staring at the bundled form of Nanny Burtoncappe. As she did, the old lady seemed to become aware of her, and stopping her croaks, raised her head. "Hello, my dear," she said. "You must be the bride, the actress girl. Come closer, I can hardly see you, *Isabella.*"

Isabella jumped in alarm. "What...what did you say? What did you call me?" She strode towards Nanny, her shoes clicking on the wooden parquet flooring. Drawing close, she could see Nanny's eyes were misted, partly blocked by cataracts.

"Your name, just your name, Arabella," chortled Nanny. "Didn't I get it right, dear? From what I can see you're very pretty, just as Augustus said in his letters to me". A little bit of spittle dampened the old woman's lips; it ran onto her pointed and whiskery chin. "Just the master's type. Fair and lithe; faerie-like. Oh, yes, faerie-like indeed. But you're not a real faerie, of course....even if you're *different.* And all the better for it. You'll be far more suitable for the Master than the last one..."

"What? I don't understand. Who is the 'last one'?"

"The last one? Didn't he tell you, Miss Arabella? Didn't the Master tell you he'd been wed before?"

"No, he did not." Isabella sat down heavily on the bed, her knees feeling suddenly weak. This information should have come as no surprise; men lost wives and remarried all the time in this era of early mortality, but it struck home how little she knew about her 'groom. It just seemed...strange...that there was an unknown, unmentioned woman before her, the former Lady of Elvingstone Manor, who may have even slept in this very room.

"Pretty she was, fine as gossamer, pale as moonlight," chirped Nanny, rocking back and forth slightly. "But cold, oh so cold. She wouldn't speak to the likes of me. No, poor old Nanny didn't even get to dress her for the wedding. She wouldn't have it. All I could do was give her something blue, that's all she would accept from me...She liked blue, she did; blue like the petals of the hydrangeas. That's where Master Augustus first spied her, you know—peering through the hydrangeas out in the arbour." Unsteadily, Nanny teetered over to an old music box that stood on the nearby dresser. It began to chime as she opened the enamelled lid. "I have her blue garter here. I'd say it's yours now."

"No, no, it was hers," said Isabella, with vehemence. "Keep it. I don't follow old traditions; after all, this wedding is hardly traditional."

Nanny shut the music box with a snap. "Aye, aye, maybe you're right. A new start, nothing of what went before."

Isabella nodded but despite herself, she wanted to know more. Just a little more. This lost wife. "Her name, what was her name?"

"An odd name it was to the ear. Blodeyn."

"Blodeyn. I have never heard another with that name. That sounds Welsh. Was she Welsh?"

"Oh, her name may have been Welsh, but I don't know her true origins, not at all! Her name was too outlandish for the Master—he made her change it. The name meant 'flower'—so she became Floralie. Much more respectable in the Master's eyes. How could he introduce his wife with a name that seemed mumbo-jumbo to most?"

"Floralie…" murmured Isabella. An image popped into her head. Flowers. A glade filled with sunset and shadows. Petals falling; cobwebs illuminated by late sun. Hydrangeas the colour of mourning blue, tear drop laden with night-dew. A girl dancing, dancing better than she could ever dance, on feet bare and white as lilies…

"Aye, that was her. So pretty, but as I said…cold. I always thought her unlucky, I'll tell you truthfully. Always thought so. Wasn't my business but I begged Master Augustus not to marry her, and there were tears and bad feelings between us. He roared at me; only time, ever…his Nanny. He wanted her. Oh, how he wanted her. Was like he was enchanted, and perhaps he was." A sly look passed over her wrinkled face. "But they were happy enough for a time… Even had a little boy, oh that poor little lad, little Aelfred."

"Aelfred! A child?" Isabella's mind raced back to the sheeted cradle she had seen so briefly in one of the rooms. "He has a child! Where…where is that child?"

"Dead," said Nanny Burtoncappe in a most plaintive voice. "Terribly tragic, Mistress Arabella. The cold iron. It was the cold iron. Mistress Floralie had told Master Augustus not to use the iron, and he didn't at first…but he got cocky, so over-confident. Thought she was exaggerating its danger. Ah, that was an awful day, so awful it was." Tears began to leak out of the lined corners of Nanny's eyes. "I'll never forget the screams, the screams. Aelfred was dead And then she went, Floralie went and was never seen again."

Cold waves of horror rushed over Isabella. "Nanny, please tell me…What do you mean by 'cold iron'? What did Augustus do that led to his son's death? Tell me, what did he do?"

But Nanny wasn't answering. She was rocking back and forth again, her half-blind eyes grown milky and unfocused, murmuring softly another segment of the song she had been singing earlier that day,

"We'll prick him, we'll prick him all over with a pin,
And that'll make my lady to come down to him.'
So he pricked him, he pricked him all over with a pin,
And the nurse held the basin for the blood to flow in…."

"Nanny, Nanny, stop, I don't want to hear," cried Isabella, pressing her hands to her ears, but the strange old woman went on singing, and gurning and grinning.

When Nanny stopped crooning her eerie song, she returned to normal, or what passed as normal for her. Then it was all clucking and cosseting as she put Isabella to bed, called the maids, Jemima and Pearl, for a hot water-bottle and a posset and combed out Isabella's hair with an abalone-shell comb. "You'll sleep well tonight," she said with an unnerving cheerfulness.

I doubt it, thought Isabella, watching the claw-like hand rise and fall with the comb.

"Do you want to see the dress, the lovely wedding dress you'll have?"

Isabella was silent for a moment. She supposed the mysterious Floralie had worn the dress too, and that made her feel uncomfortable, but she knew there would be no other dress for her. She had an arrangement, not a proper marriage to make. Short of running away into the night, into a country that was familiar and yet foreign, she was stuck with its consequences of her decision. "I suppose so," she said slowly. "Better find out if it fits."

"The dress is three hundred years old," said Nanny, shuffling over to a great, rosewood wardrobe. "The Master's mother, Lady Helena, wore it for her nuptials, and her mother before her and so on back into time."

Reaching into the wardrobe, the old woman pulled out a white dress. It was made of silk and lace and pearls, all somewhat discoloured by age. A cap with a long veil accompanied it.

"It is beautiful," Isabella had to admit. She had never envisioned being married in a gown so fine. In fact, marriage had really not been on the agenda back in the 21st century. There had been a few boyfriends, very few. One that broke her heart, one that loved football more than her…they were long gone and she'd shed all the tears she was ever going to over them.

"You will be a beautiful bride," said Nanny Burtoncappe firmly, her demeanour suddenly motherly. "Far nicer than that Floralie, if truth be told. Not so…cold…"

Isabella did not think she would sleep that night. For ages, she lay curled around the stoneware water bottle, pressing it to her shivering flesh. Nanny had ambled off to her own room and Isabella was alone, listening to every creak and groan in the huge ancient house. Passing westward, the moon hovered in the bedroom window, its pallid light casting a white streak over the floor.

Isabella tried to turn her head; in the city, she had loved to walk out with her friends after a concert or a show, with a big moon hanging overhead, winking like a friendly watchful eye over the spires of Westminster of the turrets of the Tower. The streets had buzzed with late nightlife; pubs and bars with their fogged windows, the expensive restaurants where she and her mates spent their pay cheques. This moon seemed different to the familiar old moon over London. Round, pockmarked, and wan, it almost seemed like a…a…floating severed head, a barren skull that watched with chill, empty eyes.

"Stop being silly." Isabella chided herself, huddling in the dark. "You're in a strange place, that's all. Don't start filling your own head with nonsense."

Turning over, she adjusted the quilt over herself for more warmth. Nanny had stoked a tiny fire in the tiled fireplace but it was nearly out; only a sullen ember or two burned on the hearth. The house was bone-chillingly cold. No central heating in this time.

Then Isabella heard it—a haunting sound floating through the darkness outside her window. "*Oooo…oooo.*"

She sat bolt upright, clutching the coverlet around her as the sound repeated. And then she laughed. She had clearly been in the city too long. She knew that sound from girlhood when her mother took her to visit aunts and uncles in the countryside…it was only an owl.

Swinging out of her bed, she approached the window in an attempt to see her avian tormentor. Down below, the gravel paths and the high topiary were blue-tinged in the moonlight. To her delight, she spotted the owl soaring across the star speckled sky, its white wings extended and its eyes amber and flower-like.

"May you catch your prey, old owl, and cease to trouble me with your crying," she murmured, tracking the bird's flight with her gaze. Down beside the house it flew, then along an avenue of night-clad yews that led up to a squat medieval church.

The ancient little church where she would be married at noon.

"Who would have ever thought this would happen?" she breathed, and then a gasp was torn from her lips.

A white figure, looking very much like a bride in a long gown, stood at the lych-gate near the church. White veil, white dress, white hands, white face, but the distant eyes were two black blots, like the eye sockets of a livid skull.

"No!" A cry of terror ripped from Isabella's throat and she closed her eyes against the awful vision.

A moment later, she opened her eyes again. She blinked. The white-clad figure, whatever it was, had vanished, and only the moonlight wandered along the avenue to the church.

"It was only in my head," she whispered desperately, wretchedly, and she clambered back into bed. "Ghosts don't exist." But did they? In her world of 2018, time travel did not exist either. And yet here she was in a Victorian world, with Queen Victoria firmly on the throne.

She tossed and turned, trying to forget her predicament and get just a few hours' sleep. Down below she heard Nanny start her dismal singing again:

"*Oh, the lady came downstairs, she was thinking no harm.*
Lord Lankin stood ready for to catch her in his arms.
There's blood in the kitchen,
there's blood in the hall,
there's blood in the parlour where my lady did fall."

She rolled the pillow over her head, desperate to block the hated sound. To her surprise, after a little while, with both pillow and cover over her ears, she found sleep creeping up to take her.

In the morning, the entire world seemed bright and fair. The eeriness of the darkness had faded away and Isabella lay sprawled on her back, in an ornate four-poster bed, warm and comfortable amidst goose-down pillows and embroidered quilts. Radiant sunlight shone through dusty panes of glass and dust motes danced merrily on the floorboards. The smell of cooking permeated the air, rising from the distant kitchens on the lowest floor of the manor.

Into the bedroom shuffled Nanny carrying a silver tray in her gnarled old hands. "Breakfast for the bride!"

Isabella wished there was a coffee and a croissant—her usual breakfast-but soon found herself enjoying honeyed porridge, cheese upon toast and tea. Once she was done, Nanny called for Jemima to take the tray away and Isabella was hustled into the vast blue and white china tub in the little bathroom adjacent to the bedchamber. The water, screeching and thumping through ancient metal pipes, steamed as it hit the sides of the porcelain tub.

After she had bathed, Nanny and Jemima assisted Isabella into her wedding dress, fastening the stays and ties with expert fingers. "Not too tight, I might faint!" cried Isabella, as Jemima gave one particularly hard tug to her corset.

"But, Mistress Arabella, you must be all bound in to have a decent figure!" cried Jemima, scandalised, as Isabella, gasping, pulled the corset off and threw it onto the bed.

Nanny cast Jemima a warning look. "Know don't go forgetting your place, Jemima. Mistress Arabella is *different* from other women. If she's more comfortable without, she'll go without."

Jemima reddened and bobbed a curtsey. "Sorry, Miss Arabella, I spoke out of turn, I did. I forgot London folk and theatre folk were different from the rest of us!"

"*Jemima!*" Nanny tutted, rolling her eyes. "Stop insulting our new mistress and make yourself useful. "Her hair, do her hair. My old fingers are no longer nimble enough for such fine work"

Jemima fussed with her Isabella's abundant locks. "Such pretty curls your have, begging your pardon, ma'am," she sighed, as she twisted and bound the hair in great coils about Isabella's head, threading it with jewelled clips and finishing the arrangement with an antique hairpin rimmed with pearls.

Nanny leant over and tremulously laid her dry, withered lips against Isabella's cheek. "My old eyes are not as good as they once were, but you look lovely, my dear. I have lived here several generations now and look forward to having you as mistress in my dear Augustus's home. Maybe, God willing, the empty nursery will be filled once more. Now go to the church and be united with my dearest boy."

"Aren't you coming, Nanny?" Isabella squeezed the old lady's hand. She was surprised how firm the grip was, despite Nanny's avowals that she was frail and dithery.

"I'm too frail, my sweetling. Moreover, weddings are only for the young, in my estimation. No, you go, Jemima here will accompany you and assist you with your dress." Then she leaned over, withered, leaf-dry lips brushing Isabella's cheek. "Be not afraid, *Isabella*. I will look out for you…"

Isabella jumped at the sound of her true name, spoken for the second time by the old lady. But Nanny had turned away and was rocking back and forth, humming, her eyes glazed and unfocussed.

Isabella exited the bedchamber followed by Jemima, who carried her train lopped over her arm. "Have you worked here long, Jemima?" asked Isabella, eager to get to know the servants as they would live in close proximity to each other and a good working relationship would be paramount.

Jemima shook her head. "I'm one of the youngest on staff. Been at Elvingstone a year. But my mother worked at Elvingstone before me, and my granny was a maid too. I'm from the nearby village of Washburn, just down the road. Our people have served the Stannions all the way since medieval times!"

"I wish I knew more about the locals…and the Stannions," Isabella sighed. *I wish I knew more about everything in this time…*"But there was…no opportunity to learn. Everything that happened…with Augustus…was so sudden"

"Master Augustus is like that—impulsive," said Jemima, with a blush. "If you don't mind me saying so…Look, Miss Arabella, the clock in the drawing room has only just chimed eleven.. I can teach you what I know about the Stannion history right now, if you wish. It would please the Master if you were to know about his ancestors."

Jemima gestured Isabella into the nearby hallway. Fastened to the wall by huge gilded brackets, portraits loomed, their canvasses speckled by fly dung and the faces of their subjects discoloured from the constant burning of the oil lamps that lit the mansion.

"That one." Jemima pointed to an armoured knight painted in a stiff, unnatural manner. This portrait had the plainest frame and the darkest discolouration; there was even a veneer of soot across the canvas as if it had perhaps once hung near torches rather than a lamp. "He's the oldest of the lot. Sir John Stannion. The King o' the day gave him land at Elvingstone, after Sir John revealed a treasonous plot against his life. He went on to build the first manor on the site of the older lodge but died fighting Scots in the north without havin' much time to enjoy it. Fortunately, he left one small son to carry on the Stannion line…

"Then…" She waved her hand toward a man in courtier's dress, whose long, solemn face looked worried and vexed. "That's Sir Ancelin. He became a counsellor to Henry…that's Henry who had a lot of wives, and was held in high esteem for a while, but like so many others, he fell afoul of Henry and lost his head on a trumped-up charge of treason. His body lies buried in the church near the mansion, but the family never got his head back. It was stuck up on London Bridge.".".

Isabella staring up at the careworn face of Augustus's ancestor. "An unfortunate fellow, it seems. Back the wrong horse."

"The Stannions aren't lucky people," said Jemima. "Impertinent though I might be, I must warn you, Mistress. But maybe you'll bring some much-needed luck. New blood, new luck. A new start, and all that."

"I hope so, Jemima." Isabella's smile was wan. Luck was something she had had much of, either back in modern times or now. "Before we go on…is there a portrait here of Augustus's parents by any chance?"

The maid nodded and gestured with her hand. "The one nearest the end, a bit out of the lamplight. Master Augustus doesn't like to look at it. It's Sir Godfrey Stannion and his wife Lady Helena. Sir Godfrey took over the remodelling of the house from his father; the Master finished it off and added his own touches."

Arabella walked over to the painting and stared up. "Lady Helena was very beautiful. Augustus has her eyes…so blue…" She flushed; she must not think such stupid trivial things! Her role was to stay alive with a roof over her head until she found how she could get back to her own century. And if she couldn't… A sudden wave of fear overtook her; tears pricked her eyes.

Clearly unaware of Isabella's distress, Jemima chuntered on, "Aye, Lady Helena was a beauty all right; she was an artist's model before she married. It's so sad to think of what happened to her. So sad."

"What happened?" Isabella wiped her eyes as she suppressed a shudder; a deep gloom seemed to have fallen over the corridor of portraits.

"Drowned in the lake, Mistress Arabella, while boating with Master Augustus's little sister Pomona. The poor mite died too. Sir Godfrey never got over it. I don't think Master Augustus ever did neither, although he pretends."

Isabella fell silent, continuing to stare at the huge, framed portrait of Lady Helena. Somewhere a clock ticked—loud, regular, like the beating of a giant heart. What curse had descended on this unfortunate family? What had she got into?

Jemima broke the uneasy silence. "Enough musings on sad old times," she said with forced cheerfulness. "Let's look to a happier future, Mistress Arabella! It's time to be getting you to the church! Wait here—I will fetch your bouquet."

The maid raced down the corridor, holding up her heavy black-and-white skirt, then swiftly returned clutching a massive bouquet of blood-red roses mingled with white lilies. "These have just been delivered from the gardens," she said with pride.

"Lilies," said Isabella in dismay.

"Don't you like them? The Master chose the flowers himself."

"They are beautiful," said Isabella, not wishing to sound ungrateful, "but are lilies not seen more often at funerals than weddings?"

"Master Augustus has…different tastes," said Jemima, looking slightly crestfallen. "You'll need to get used to it, pardon me saying so, Mistress. Now you hold those pretty flowers out front of you—yes, that's right, and I'll adjust your veil and train. There…Perfect! A true blushing bride and a great lady, mistress of Elvingstone estate! Now you start to walk, all graceful like, and I'll carry your train as if you were a princess. It's a pity, though, that you don't have proper bridesmaids to attend you, but ah well…"

Again, Jemima's words made Isabella uncomfortably aware of the oddness of her pending nuptials. Dead men's lilies, more commonly found placed on tombs. A housemaid instead of gaily-dressed bridesmaids. A groom who was near enough a stranger, albeit a mysterious and handsome one.

A groom who must have died almost a hundred years before she was born

Together Isabella and Jemima exited the manor house, passing down the Hall of Mirrors, where the age-warped glass made weird, distorted reflections; an elongated head for Jemima, the points on her maid's headdress radiating like points on a crown; a long, crying face for Isabella, resembling a distorted theatrical mask with mouth downturned. She glanced away, appalled.

Outside the mansion's front door, sunlight was beating on the gravelled path. A stately procession of precisely two, Isabella and Jemima walked down the path, watched only by rooks in the nearby topiary and by the wizened face of Nanny Burtoncappe peering from behind a curtain in an upstairs room. The rising wind lifted Isabella's flimsy veil and fluttered her train, seeking to rip the fine, threadbare lace from Jemima's hands.

This dress is like a shroud, Isabella thought suddenly, another wave of fear and panic sluicing over her. Where had such ghastly thought come from? Desperately she tried to thrust such musings from her mind, to think on the potential joys of her new life as Lady of the Manor. Even though impoverished, at Elvingstone there would be no nights without food on the table or coal in the fireplace. If she played her part, she would never want again…

But she also might never be free of this place; might never see 'home' as mundane and sometimes lonely as home had been…

The pathway was reaching an end. A wider lane took over, filled with deep puddles from last night's rain. An avenue of yews, bending in the breeze, ran in a straight line toward a solid, yellow, stone church, with an ancient sundial affixed to the side.

"St Michael's," Jemima informed her. "Where most of the Stannions have been baptised, wed and buried since the 14th century."

The two women passed under the lychgate, the corpse-gate where coffins would briefly rest on their final journey to the grave, then slid between moss-festooned tombstones decorated with sinister cherubs and winged skulls. Entering the church porch, Isabella was confronted by Romanesque pillars and fearsome carved grotesques that seemed more pagan than Christian. An usher in a black suit held open the door, hewn from a single slab of ancient oak, and Isabella entered the nave of the church to the sound of an organ playing a thunderous rendition of the wedding march. Deeper in tone than was usual and played slowly by an unskilled organist, the song took on an ominous sound rather than a merry one.

The church was dim; its small windows were remnants from an earlier structure, more like the arrow-slits one might see in a castle. Candles lit the aisle, nave and chancel, flames flickering eerily. Along the walls were many Stannion memorials—that of Sir John, lying in an alcove, a white effigy with his feet resting on a stone lion, his war banner, half-eaten by moths, draped above his resting spot; Sir Ancelin, in a decorated tomb-chest small enough for a headless man; and the plain red granite block of Augustus's parents' sepulchre resting beside the awful, tiny memorial to the lost child, Pomona. Carved in finest alabaster, the little girl was depicted lying asleep upon a cushion, her thumb in her mouth. The candles surrounding her were set into cups of deep violet glass, which cast a soft, muted colour onto the tomb.

Isabella could not fail but notice that the church was empty, save for Augustus Stannion, standing like a statue before the altar, an aged priest who looked near as decrepit as Nanny Burtoncappe, Carver the butler with his droopy, hangdog face, and a few ushers who looked ill at ease.

Bile harsh upon her tongue, she walked resolutely to join the strange man who would become her lawful wedded husband. A husband in name only.

The ceremony was mercifully brief. The priest, almost dwarfish in size, his head bald and his mouth void of teeth, mumbled in Latin; the Stannions, it seemed, had kept their Catholic Faith. No doubt, that's why poor old Sir Ancelin lost his head in the 1500's. Head bowed, Isabella murmured replies to the customary lines. Freezing sweat ran between her shoulder blades. Beside her, Augustus looked like a statue carved from ice. His voice, however, as he made the time-honoured replies to the priest, was firm, ringing down the nave of the church.

Then an usher brought the ring upon a pillow a green satin. Cold, oh so cold and tight, it was thrust upon Arabella's trembling finger.

Till death do us part.

Till death…

The organ boomed out in a deafening roar, shaking the ancient stained glass windows of St Michael's church.

Isabella, 21ST century photographer, was now Mistress Stannion, wife to a Victorian landowner.

As the organ played on, Augustus led Isabella from St Michael's church. The few who had attended the service slipped away and the bridal couple were left alone in the lane, with the yew trees bending and sweeping in the wind.

Face grave, Augustus turned to his bride. "There is something I must show you, Arabella. And things I must tell you."

Taking her arm, he led her toward another part of the churchyard, separated from the rest by a low, scruffy hedge and a corroded iron fence. A little spring burbled in a hollow near the hedge, the hawthorn above it decked in ribbons, some faded and tattered, some bright and new.

A cloutie tree, Isabella thought as the rags danced before her in the breeze. *An old country tradition asking the spirit of the well for help…*

Passing by the spring and through the gate in the fence, Augustus guided his new wife towards a second enclosure, fronted by a dark, thorny hedge. An entrance had been hacked through the greenery, and as they approached, Isabella could see the hump of a large earthen mound, its sides green with unmown grass. On the top loomed a marble angel, eyes turned skyward, hands clasped in prayer. Several fingers had broken off and some vandal had carved a date and name into the stony shoulder. Below the angel's plinth was a pair of wide, rusty red doors leading into the heart of the artificial hillock.

"What is this place?" Isabella felt hairs on the back of her neck prickle.

"Once a crypt for the junior branches of the Stannion family, and for their beloved retainers and even their mistresses. But also, deep inside, the ancient heart of Elvingstone," said Augustus enigmatically, and reaching inside his waistcoat he drew out a little phial Isabella instantly recognised. *The blood*! *Hubbard's blood*! She had almost forgotten about Augustus siphoning off the blood of his fallen opponent.

"What are you going to do with that?" she whispered, nodding toward the phial with its clotted contents. She felt as if ice had engulfed her body; the wind roared, whipping her shroud-like wedding garb.

In silence, Augustus removed the stopper from the phial. Kneeling, he let the blood run from the container into a little hollow before the rusty doors.

"I…I don't understand what you are doing!" Isabella's brows drew together in a frown. Her stomach churned. "This is abhorrent. I shan't be party to such…"

"You'll do what I damn well tell you. You're my wife now." Augustus flung down the phial, which shattered into fragments on the ground. A few stray flecks of Hubbard's blood flew up to dapple Arabella's wedding gown with lurid red spots. "You're mine, and will do as I bid. And you must know the truth about this place and what goes on here…for your own safety!"

"If there is something I need to know, then you must explain it to me. You cannot present me with riddles and half-truths and expect me to be satisfied with that!" Isabella's 21st century mores raced to the fore. "You must understand, Augustus, that I…I am not the type of women to sit about knitting and acting like she hasn't got a brain in her head! I am not going to faint or get the vapours if you are honest with me…In fact, I *want* you to be honest with me, always!"

Augustus caught her shoulders, fingers biting through the thin fabric of her wedding dress. "I will tell you then… Some of it sounds so mad, I dared not say it before, lest I be thought a lunatic straight out of Bedlam! But suffice it to say, Elvingstone is…*haunted*. Not by ghosts, no, not the spirits of human dead, but by *other* beings."

"Other beings? What do you mean by 'other beings'? She wanted to scream 'I don't believe in the supernatural' but bit down hard on her tongue.

She couldn't shout such a thing when she had somehow travelled backwards in time...

Augustus took a deep breath; it rasped between his teeth. "When man first claimed this land, *others* had dwelt here before him, unseen. He pushed them aside with his firelight and bright weapons, but they never left, just became...*hidden*. And those still dwelling here have grown strong and now make demands—for hundreds of years, they have demanded a tithe from the Stannion family. For many years, they simple offerings have placated them...like the one I gave. Lately, though, they grow restive with or without the offerings I make."

"These...these *things* require blood? What takes blood offerings?" She wanted to say 'vampires' but decided he wouldn't understand what she was talking about.

"The Old Ones." Augustus's face grew pale, his eyes unfocused and full of bitter memories. "Would I had never been born to the cursed Stannion family. They have taken everything...My wife Floralie...God, how I loved her but I should never have married her. My son...."

"They *took* your son? I thought he was dead...."

"He is dead indeed, at least upon this earth. " A spasm of pain and anger crossed Augustus's visage. "He does not lie with his near ancestors within the walls of the church, as I wished. He is..." He pointed to the iron doors, frowning, sinister, the colour of dried blood. "He lies in there."

The wind rose in a great shriek, sending dandelion spores whirling upwards in ghostly white clouds. Isabella stared at Augustus Stannion in horror, and clutching her skirts in clawed hands, fled from the graveyard.

Behind her, the church bells tolled out a funereal knell.

What, in heaven's name, had she got herself into?

Shaking from head to toe, Isabella hid in her bedchamber. What had she just witnessed? What had Augustus told her?

"What have I done?" she cried, heart hammering against her ribs. "I...I should have stayed in London...at the theatre. Maybe if I fell through into this time, I could fall backwards. Oh God..."

Frantically, she began to pace the room, the floorboards creaking under her light tread. She was legally Augustus Stannion's wife, and now she was shut behind high walls. There was no way she could get a message to the outside world without him finding out—and who would believe her tale or even care for her fate? Not in this strict era. She knew what they would say—she had made her bed, now she must lie in it.

Tormented, she pressed sticky hands to her feverish brow. What could be wrong with Augustus, to behave in such a manner and to believe such wild fantasies? He must be a lunatic who had only escaped the asylum because of his rank and family name.

And yet, she had a hard time comparing him to the tragic creatures her alter ego Arabella had sometimes seen escaping from the Bedlam Hospital, shrieking and whooping as they careered along the streets in their prisoner's garb whilst officials chased them with restraints in hand.

Maybe, whatever afflicted Augustus could be banished. Maybe she was the one who could cast out the demons that clearly ate at him...She was not a mental health professional but she's read enough pop psychology to maybe help a little.

"But why should I?" she breathed, and then she flushed. As much as she would have liked to deny it, from the moment she met her Augustus, there had been a frisson of attraction. No, more than just a 'frisson.' She felt more attracted to him to him than any man she had ever met. What woman wouldn't want someone akin to Mr Darcy in looks and manners, after all?

She stared out of the window; dusk was falling, blue and sorrowful. Leaning on the sill, she stared toward the church, where that very day she became an unhappy bride, and towards the sombre graveyard attached to it. To her dismay, she fancied she saw lights, glimmering like glowworms' trails but much larger, circling around and around the mounded crypt with its sorrowful angel and rusted doors...

"No, this is foolishness!" she cried and tore her gaze away.

Down below, in the drawing room with its vast gold painted columns, suits of armour and décor of jesters and jugglers, a piano began to tinkle, playing a country air both haunting and melodic. Suddenly, though, whoever played began to crash on the keys with brutal force, making a strident cacophony that caused Isabella to wince and press her hands to her ears.

No servant would dare make such discordant noise in his master's home, she was sure of that—therefore, the pianist had to be Augustus. Augustus, mad and raging, going from calm to crazed.

She was trapped, and she was his wife, for better or for ill...

She began to laugh bitterly while tears leaked out of the corner of her eyes and fell in shining drops, streaking the worn fabric of the ancestral bride's gown and mingling with the red dots of Hubbard's blood.

And then she heard the mad music cease in the room below. Footsteps sounded on the stairs, rang through the hallways. A man's heavy tread. Augustus was coming...to claim his bride.

This was what you bought into, you idiot! Isabella's mind screamed at her. *He's an 19th century male! He promised he was only after a marriage of convenience but he was lying...taking advantage! You're bound to him in holy matrimony, and he can do what he likes to you with no recourse! You were a fool, fool, turned by a handsome face and the idea of a comfortable life. He's going to rape you, and you will have no recourse...*

The bedchamber door creaked open. Cold drafts from the hall flooded in, making the candles and lanterns dip and sway. Augustus stood there, hatless and without his jacket. His starched white shirt hung open to his waist. The smell of gin clung to him—he was clearly drunk.

Isabella froze, a rabbit caught in the transfixing glare of a hungry snake.

"Do not be afraid," Augustus slurred. "You look so fearful. Why would I hurt you? Why would I? I've never willingly hurt anyone."

"You…you're drunk!" Isabella's voice emerged a prim squeak. She cursed herself inwardly. She want to sound authoritative.

"Just enjoyed a wedding tipple—without my goddamn wife, I might add," he suddenly snarled.

"Don't…don't shout!" Isabella backed up, surreptitiously reaching for one of the candleholders on the dresser, to use as a weapon if need be. "You promised me you would not raise your hand or voice to me! I thought you were a man of your word! If you…you touch me, Augustus…you are no…no gentleman!"

He calmed instantly, although he still staggered towards her. "I did not mean to frighten you; I am a man of honour. I would not harm a lady, especially my wife…Especially…"

He collapsed before her kneeling like a supplicant before a monarch. "Forgive me, Arabella. Forgive me!"

"I…I do. Oh please, get up! Get up!"

Augustus lurched to his feet, and suddenly his arm looped around her waist, drawing him against his muscled torso. She felt the heat from him burning into flesh, bones. "Let out your hair," he breathed. "I want to see your hair! How I despise these fashions that keep a woman's hair tied up or concealed by a hat! Let it out!"

"No…not, I don't think that's wise in your present state!" she insisted, holding up her hands defensively. "You need to sober up, Augustus, and think what you are doing."

He ignored her and with shaking fingers, snatched at the jewelled pins holding the coils and curls of her hair in place. Thick, auburn-tinted locks tumbled down her back, gleaming in the wavering light.

Augustus's breathing deepened. "So like…so like, though her hair was raven's wing dark," he muttered. "And the face, so alike…and yet…yet…"

In a passion, he grabbed her; she clawed at the candlestick but it fell from her shaking fingers and clattered away. Augustus' eyes were staring, glazed. "Have you come back? Come back in a different form to toy with me? I beg you, no more tortures! The iron, the bloody iron; I was an idiot, I believed it was just a myth. Folklore. I would have never harmed you, or Aelfred. Never. Oh, Floralie, my girl of flowers, forgive me my many sins towards you…"

A painful gasp broke from Isabella's lips. He thought she was the spirit of his dead wife, Floralie! She began to struggle in his crushing embrace. "I am not her, I'm not Floralie! I won't pretend to be her so that you can expiate your guilt in some disgusting way!"

Augustus fell back from her, nearly losing his footing in his drunken state. "No, no, you are right. I have acted mad, a fool. I cannot, dare not touch you. I brought you to Elvingstone only so that men's cruel tongues would cease to flap; there were enough rumours about me as it was, without my long-unmarried state being the subject of discussion. I have behaved abominably towards you. I do not normally imbibe to excess. I will leave this room at once and not re-enter unbidden ever again. We should both try to forget it happened, and tomorrow progress as civilised folk with the business arrangement that is our marriage."

He tried to make a small bow, nearly toppling over in his inebriated state. "I bid you goodnight, Mistress Arabella."

He staggered for the door, knocking over several candles in his wake. Crying out, Isabella leapt at the falling tapers, beating out their small flames with her hands in case they caught on her dress or the filmy draperies overhanging the bed. A few feet from her face, the door slammed, the impact shaking the doorframe. Tears leaked from her eyes once again as she gathered up the fallen candles, uncaring that the hot wax burnt her fingertips.

Her wedding night.

Her folly.

Her fate.

Chapter Five: The Lake

Summer passed. Isabella began to take on duties around the Elvingstone estate, guided by Nanny and Jemima—dealing with accounts, seeing the servants' wages were paid, writing letters. Augustus stalked around the estate, a tall thin figure in his tight breeches and ruffled shirt, but he said little to his erstwhile wife. He was coldly courteous, showing no signs of the drunken passion he had displayed on their wedding night. No mentions were made of his lost wife Floralie, or of *them*…the unearthly beings he claimed lived within the mound in the graveyard.

As for the 'beings', Isabella still saw lights near the church every now and then, and once in a thunderstorm, she thought she had seen a rider upon a great stallion mingled with the conflagration in the sky, wielding a spear that pierced the roiling clouds. However, she fought back the urge to believe such a vision was real, and ducked under the bedcovers every night mumbling half-forgotten prayers she had not uttered since childhood.

But when she found sleep, there would be dreams, bad dreams, or dreams of a home that seemed lost to her, and she would awake, shaking and sobbing, and Nanny Burtoncappe, as if she knew, would open the door and fumble in on arthritic feet, and feed her warm milk in a tall, fluted glass and stroke her hair. "It is as it was meant to be, Arabella," she said. "Pretty little Bella. He will need you, you know."

"Really, Nanny?" said Isabella. "You may be old but you are not stupid, are you? You know we are not…as normal man and wife."

"All things in their time, my dear." Nanny grinned. "Time can be a funny old thing, bringing things to the way they should be."

"I don't understand."

"Don't you, Miss Bella? I think you do. Or will before long…."

As the leaves began to turn on the trees in the parkland, drifting like tiny curled boats upon the lake where Augustus's mother and sister had drowned, Augustus called Isabella into his smoking room, a small, darkly panelled chamber attached to his private bedroom. Deep red gemstones affixed in the single, stained glass window allowed in a ruddy light that spread over his desk, the unlit lamps, the exotic designs on the imported Turkish. The smell of tobacco and wax hung heavy in the air, along with the fragrance Augustus wore—frankincense, musk. A little clock in a glass dome ticked loudly on the mantle above the grated fireplace; its face was rather sinister, graven with the image of an old man bearing a scythe—Father Time.

Isabella suppressed a shudder as her gaze fixed on the clock face. Time…what had it done to her? Unasked, she had done what millions wished for—time travel, an entrance to the past. But what had it brought her? Years of loneliness, locked behind the walls and gates of a rich man's estate?

"You look a bit pale," Augustus said, in a matter of fact manner. "May I enquire as to your health?"

"I…I have not been out much of late. I spend much of my days reading or visiting the church." It was true; she walked out most morning to St Michael's, trailing down the yew-aisle, where winds whispered like mocking ghosts, and passing under the lychgate where so many coffins had lain. She would then enter the empty church, with its stale incense and grave mould reek, and look at the tattered banners of Stannions long dead or lay hands on the cold stone tombs: the knight, the headless statesman, the drowned child….

But she never entered the adjacent yard with the hummock faced by rusty gates, never walked beyond the pleasant green well with its fluttering rag-tributes. While she took some comfort in medieval stone and ancestral Stannion bones, the forebears of her unloving husband, she felt a wall separating her from the mound, a protective unseen barrier keeping her from …*what?*

"You are not happy here."

"Happy enough," she lied, not wishing to appear weak or nagging. A deal was a deal. And if Augustus turned her out, where would she go? How would she survive in an England nearly as alien as the moon? "I will not lie, though…I miss the city. I miss London."

His right eyebrow crooked. "Truly? You miss working with raddled old harridans like that Eulalia creature, who imagine they are more than they are and treat you like scum? You miss working for a pittance and living in a hovel, the prey of the unscrupulous?"

Is that how you saw me—'prey'? Am I your prey, Augustus Stannion?
"Those things were the downside of my profession, but yes, yes, I do miss parts of my old life. I also miss the costumes and the dancing, the camaraderie backstage." She didn't miss those things, but somewhere within her, whatever had been Arabella Lorne stirred, her twin in spirit. She knew what Arabella had loved.

.Augustus leant back into his carved oak chair and stared out the high window. The red light from the translucent bauble in the glass reflected off the high planes of his face; turned the surfaces of his eyes to blood. "Well, I have some good news for you, then, Arabella."

Isabella's heart leapt into her mouth. Was he going to ask her to leave? Say he wanted a divorce? Did he regret their unorthodox marriage? "What is this good news?" She strove to keep the tremble from her voice.

He cleared his throat. "For nigh on a hundred years, the Stannions have held a ball in the grounds of the manor. Invitations are sent to my acquaintances from the city, my former business partners, my kin from afar demesnes, and all those who serve the household or live within a league of the estate. In the past, the ball was a grand affair, but sadly, in the past few years, I allowed its splendour to dwindle; due to the sorrows of my existence, I was in no mood for festivities. A drink and a cake were all the attendees received; they must have thought me a miser! I want to change that unfortunate impression—it is time for the Stannion name to take precedence once more."

"I have no experience in running such an event!"

"No, I did not expect that you did. But you are of a theatrical bent, and I have decided it shall be a fancy dress ball."

Isabella's face brightened. Costumes and fun! How long it seemed since she'd heard music or danced!

"Will there be dancing, Augustus?"

"Of course there will be dancing! Lots of it, out on the lawns, weather permitting."

Isabella could not help herself; she impulsively flung her arms around Augustus' neck, nearly overbalancing him. A shock went through her as her hands descended on the broad shoulders; she felt his hot breath on her cheek, saw his eyes darken…was it with distrust or with desire? "Oh thank you, Augustus, I would be delighted to help with the arrangements. I am so thrilled that I shall be able to dance again."

Augustus shifted in his seat; his mouth moved, lips turning up in a small smile. She had seldom seen him smile. "I…I will be glad to see you dance again, Arabella." His hand crept out, clasped hers, rolling her wedding band between his fingertips in an almost intimate motion. She felt an unexpected rush of heat run through her. She had not expected any physical contact…nor had she expected to be the first to instigate it. What was wrong with her? But Augustus Stannion was no longer a stranger…

As abruptly as Augustus's flash of warmth came, it vanished. His face assumed its normal glacial hauteur. He released her hand and swivelled away from her, head low over his desk, reaching for a quill pen. "I must commence with business now, Arabella. I will leave the details of the masked Ball in your no doubt capable hands. Nanny and Jemima will have a guest list for the invitations; they will also give you ideas on the food, drink and decorations that we will need."

"I will need some details, Augustus? When do you plan to hold this Ball?"

The nib of Augustus's pen scratched on the parchment. He paused, a blot forming, then glanced up, expression unreadable. "The traditional day for the Grand Ball is October 31. Halloween."

Isabella felt an icy shiver run down her spine. Halloween was a day of kids, black cats, and American candy in the 21st century...but its significance in the 19th? All Saints and All Souls, resting over the old Celtic feast day of Samhain.

September had arrived, with cooler, crisper weather and the first touch of night-frost on flowerbeds and lawns. Blue skies still abounded, but the leaves were turning gold and red, drifting down from trees in the park—save for the great aisle of Yew trees by St Michael's church that remained forever dark and ominous, summer and winter. Isabella's daily walks to the lake brought new, unexpected pleasures as she took the air, rich with the scent of distant wood-smoke and discussed minutiae of the upcoming Ball with Jemima.

"Are all the invitations sent?" She thought of the cards she had chosen for the occasion; white with gold, embossed lettering in Gothic script

"Yes, ma'am," replied Jemima. "We've had some acceptances already. Those in the village on the general invite say they are coming; I asked around after church last Sunday."

"What about the food? Will we have enough to satisfy everyone? It is such a pity we are living in rather straightened circumstances here at Elvingstone."

"There are plenty who owe plenty to the Stannions, though, Mistress Arabella," said Jemima. "I've been speaking to them in the town, seeing what can be donated for the Ball. We have a big, tiered cake coming from Mrs Humble, the baker, and Grimes the fishmonger is donating some pike and cod, too. Our own stock of salt beef is not insubstantial, and the dairy still produces wholesome cheese. Sir Augustus has kept the wine cellar well-filled; there are many bottles of excellent vintage, some over a hundred years old."

"We need more, though—poultry, pork, lamb. A variety of things."

"You leave it to me, Mistress. I know lots of folk who'd gladly donate a chicken or two just to get a look at the Manor grounds."

"Is the Ball—and Elvingstone—truly such a draw?"

"Oh yes, Mistress; with all the legends and rumours..." She halted suddenly by the lakeside, staring at her toes.

Isabella stopped in her tracks and eyed the maid suspiciously. "What legends are those? Do tell me, Jemima."

"Oh, oh…" Jemima seemed flustered. "You know, the usual sort of nonsense. Ghosts and ghouls. Old Stannion holding his head under his arm. The Elves…"

"Elves? You mean like those in children's stories? Little manikins with pointed ears that sit under toadstools? How ludicrous!" Isabella let out a harsh laugh. Oddly, the mention of fairytale creatures made her feel rattled and uncomfortable. Augustus had spoken about unearthly beings on the estate…

Jemima shook her head with a violent motion, almost dislodging her prim cap. Her cheeks had paled; her expression was one of unease. "These Elves ain't like the storybook ones, oh no. They are tall; sometimes they appear as beams of light eight-foot tall! Some shine silver and some shine gold, and they glow like the moon and the sun. Their singing is fair as that of the angels and if they catch you, they can make you dance for a hundred years and not stop till your feet are worn to nubs."

"And where do these 'Elves' live?" said Isabella. She wanted to mock, she wanted to jeer…but she could not. She feared, she suspected…

Jemima licked her dry lips; her hands twisted nervously in her white apron. "Don't you know, Mistress? Can't you guess? They live in the mound, the great mound."

"What mound?" Isabella's voice was a whisper.

"The Stannion crypt in the churchyard, of course. When the Stannions decided the church was too full for burials of their favourites, they dug into what they thought was a natural hillock in the churchyard. Found some old pots and bones but threw them aside. They built their own sepulchre using the ancient one as a base for it, but it seems they opened a portal when they did. A portal to the Otherworld. Some might say a portal to Hell!"

"That's lunatic's talk!" hissed Isabella. "You must forget you ever said it, Jemima! There is but one world and we live in it." *Even if we are out of our own time…*

"But, Mistress Arabella, it's true, I swear it is!" Jemima's eyes flashed with sudden anger and her hands curled into balls at her side. "If you don't respect the Lordly People, they can bring you great harm. Master Augustus found that out, to his cost! He knows all about them, none better! You ask him!"

"Jemima, be quiet! You have no right to criticise the Master for anything he has done or to tell me to bother my husband with nonsense. Enough of that has gone on at Elvingstone, it seems. Elves! We are supposed to be in the…the Age of Reason!"

Jemima's mouth worked. At length, her voice emerged, low and shaking with anger. "Well, you may consider me a country bumpkin, but I know what I've seen. I'd say your years of city living have blinded you, Mistress Arabella. Blinded you to the truth."

"You are becoming most rude!" Isabella frowned at the maid. It made her uncomfortable to tell someone off for their opinion, but she was wise enough to know if she didn't play the part of upper-class Victoria housewife, the servants would not respect her—might even turn against her. Kindness would be seen as weakness. "I am dismissing you from my presence the rest of the day. Go to the house and make yourself useful in the scullery."

"As you wish, Mistress." Sour-faced and pouting, Jemima dropped an awkward curtsey then hurried towards the mansion without looking back.

Isabella pressed her hands to her forehead. Her temples had begun to throb furiously. How had she managed to turn a pleasant walk and a discussion of the upcoming Ball into an argument? But she had no desire to listen to old wives' tales and dark local lore. Why? She stared at her feet, in their soft silk shoes. Because she was afraid. Crushingly afraid. She did not believe in fairies and pixies but something did seem amiss at Elvingstone. As amiss as her journey through time. As the saying went, '*there is more in heaven and earth…*'

Dolefully, she continued to walk around the periphery of the lake, past the old, gnarled stones that marked the path, through the trees with their gold-hued leaves. On her left, the waters of the lake, fringed by reeds, dappled by water lilies, were a clear blue, mirroring the pale October sky. There was no wind.

Suddenly a cold blast of air came sailing down the path, frigid as if deepest December had unexpectedly arrived at Elvingstone. Leaves were torn off the trees and flung to the ground; they caught in Isabella's hair which, torn free from its pins, streamed out in the unexpected gale.

A mist began to rise on the shore of the lake, and suddenly the waters became rippled and grey. Isabella raised her face to the sky, perturbed by the abrupt change in the weather; to her shock, it was still blue, cloudless and serene.

"This is impossible!" she cried. "The lake should mirror the sky, yet the water has gone dark as if a storm brewed above. But there is no storm!"

Her voice fell flat amidst the leaves. She could hear rustling, chuckling all around her in the ferns, the briars, the birches. Down the path, in the wake of the first frigid blast of wind, a pale mist began to roll, tumbling in swells over ruts in the ground, reaching out in tendrils towards her like thin, bony fingers. In the heart of the mist, she spied a female figure clad in a long gown, shroud-ragged, bone-bleached. "Arabella…" She heard her name called, and then, "*Oh, Isabella…*"

Unknown panic gripped her. Yanking up her skirts to avoid tripping, she started to run. The wind rose in a howl. The temperature dropped. The trees of the lakeshore dipped and slashed at her with their boughs, almost as if they had burst into malign life. Puffball mushrooms exploded, showering her with spores. A murder of crows darted between the trees, surrounding her, battering her with their wings before sailing away into a growing gloom.

"Isabella…why do you run? Do you not want to greet me? To meet me? Don't you wonder who I am?" The white-clad woman's voice grew louder, mocking.

Isabella dared not glance over her shoulder for fear of what she might see. She started to run faster, adrenalin surging through her body, her heart hammering so hard she feared it might explode. The wind gave out another terrifying shriek. Crystals of ice dashed into her face. In the lake, the reeds were wilting, dying, shrivelling up before her eyes. Black oiliness streaked across the choppy surface as the greenery decayed and disintegrated. Frogs started to exit the water, hopping across her path in a panic. In the woods, a horn could be heard blowing—a huntsman's horn. Hounds began to yammer, or was it migrating geese high above in the sky? She did not know. All she knew was that she was the hunted.

She had reached the far end of the boating lake. No one visited this end of the park anymore; weeds and briars tangled over the trail, tearing her skirts as she rushed by. A ruined boathouse stood on the edge of the water, trees sprouting through its decayed fabric. St Elmo's fire played around the windows with their shattered panes of glass.

Panting, Isabella flung herself through the boathouse's open door. Inside, the place stunk of mould and green, gelid water. Light shone through gaps in the roof where storms had torn tiles away. Hastily she rooted around seeking a weapon amidst the fallen beams—but what sort of a weapon could she use on the unseen enemy, for she knew instinctively it held malice towards her, that followed her through the woods?

Suddenly her gaze fell upon a little wooden rowboat, dragged up onto wooden pilings. Its paint was grey and peeling, but it had no visible damage. A splintering paddle lay beside it on the ground.

Grabbing the paddle, Isabella thrust it against the boat's prow, pushing it towards the open front of the boathouse. It rocked and almost overturned as it came off the pilings, then it began to slide slowly but steadily towards the lapping water.

Behind Isabella, the unnatural gale battered the boathouse. The St Elmo's fire in the windows died with a hiss. Mist crept up in its place, seeping through chinks in the ruinous walls.

Isabella could wait no longer; terror enveloped her in a dark cloud. With a cry, she pushed the boat out into the waves and blundered after it, up to her knees in filthy water, still clutching the paddle in one hand. Muscles wrenched and tore as she struggled to heave herself into the boat.

The wind was still ascending, shrieking its fury through the trees. In the back of the boathouse a figure appeared, glowing, incandescent, arms outstretched. "Bella...Ara...Isa, why will you not meet me? Why do you fear me so?"

Isabella paddled with fury, ignoring the pain that shot through arms and shoulders. The rowboat bobbed out into the swell, prow turning toward the far side of the lake, where gardeners had cleared the trees and manicured lawns ran up to the golden-grey bulk of the manor.

"Isabella..." the voice behind her called, mocking, plaintive. "You need to see me...to heed me...We have so much in common. So much! And I know your secret, I know so much of importance to you..."

Isabella's head craned around, almost as if she were being forced to look at her pursuer against her will. On the water's edge floated the white figure, hair mingled with mist, fog-streamers exuding from below the trailing skirts.

And its face was hers.

Oh, yes, there were small differences, the features sharper, more refined, the ears slightly peaked through the strands of long raven hair, and the eyes crackled with blue fire; the leavings of lightning. But otherwise, the resemblance was remarkable. Eerie. Unnatural.

The figure raised its arms, billowing mist; the azure flames darted from the cold, glittering eyes, lighting the gloom that had fallen over the lake. "Don't you want to know my name, Isabella? Don't you? Augustus Stannion called me…Floralie."

Isabella flailed her paddle in the water, trying to get away.

Floralie stood smiling, white death, a ghoul that bore her own face. "We could come to an agreement, you and I. I want Augustus; you do not. I could send you home, away from this time that is not yours. Wouldn't you like that…to leave this time?"

Isabella ceased her frantic paddling. Plucking up her courage, she called back at the glowing spectres, "Why do you want Augustus? He said you abandoned him! And if I went back to modern London, what would happen to this body I inhabit…Arabella Lorne?"

The white, glowing shoulder lifted in a shrug. "I want him for revenge. You do not understand how much I hate him. As for the body you inhabit, yours and yet not yours…it would die; you are the dominant power…it is just a host. But why would you care? Arabella Lorne was just another addle-pated girl with foolish dreams of grandeur. In your world, she was a long time old bones in an unmarked grave!"

Isabella went cold. She could not trust this frightening, cynical creature, whatever she was. "I reject you!" she cried. "Keep away from me…and Augustus Stannion!"

Floralie flung back her head and laughed; ice pellets sprayed from her mouth like crystalline vomit. "You fool! You want Stannion more than you admit! Go then…go…fly before me in your sad little boat. A special little boat that, long ago doomed those who rode in it!"

Isabella felt the boat beneath her buck as if moved by a giant, unseen hand. Then it was cast forward into heaving waves that grew tall as mountains; jagged grey peaks limned with preternatural light. Releasing the paddle, she clawed at the sides of the boat, struggling to keep her grip. The gale shrieked around her, malevolent, a living thing, and sent her tiny craft swinging in circles. Leaves torn from the trees struck her face, stinging her eyes. The lake surface was transformed into a giant whirlpool, trying to suck her down into its depths.

Desperately she clung to the boat as it rocked and bucked, timbers groaning as they threatened to break apart.

"You can't escape, Isabella," whispered the apparition that bore her face. "The spirits of the past will take you, consume you…"

The water ceased to swirl and boil. Out of the depths, an arm lifted, greenish- white, mottled, bloated. It looped over the prow of Isabella's boat, causing it to tilt alarmingly to one side.

"No," Isabella cried in horror, flinging herself forward to beat at the arm. The flesh was slimy, rancid, melting from the bone. She recoiled in revulsion, and in that instant, the hand shot out and grasped her gown, dragging her from the boat into the water.

Coldness rushed through her, chilling her to the core. Blinded, she flopped and thrashed, her heavy Victorian skirts beginning a long, deathly, downwards trek. She could feel hands touching her, pulling her towards a watery grave. She forced her eyes open; through the pain, she saw a woman, a dead woman, floating below, face half-decayed, teeth grinning through shreds of flesh. Her hair twirled up like waterweeds in a rank green cloud. Beside her, clinging to her waist, was a dead child, thumb in her mouth, suffused face ballooned in death, her hair a mass of snarled elflocks filled with leaves.

Augustus's mother and his sister, Pomona, who died in a boating accident on the lake!

"It can't be!" Isabella screamed inwardly. "They are no longer in the lake. They are buried in St Michael's church. This is just…just an *ILLUSION*!"

The last word burst from her lips in a great rush. Water poured into her mouth but at the same time, she gave a great kick, dislodging the grim lych that clawed at her skirts. The skirts tore as the grotesque creature fell away, and Isabella burst up onto the lake's surface, gasping for air and flailing her arms. Below her, she could see the two corpses, motionless now, whirling down toward the murk of the lakebed, looking ever more and more like two rotted chunks of wood and less like human bodies as they descended into the depths.

The unnatural storm was still raging on the surface, however. Isabella had not swum since she was a child, but she struck out with all her remaining energy. On the bank, by the boathouse, she heard the laughter of her doppelganger. "This is my territory, Isabella, and has been for untold thousands of years. You won't escape."

Suddenly on the farthest shore, the treeless one nearest to the mansion, Isabella spotted a figure running madly down the green lawns towards the water's edge. "Help me, help me!" she screamed, waving her arm in a frantic motion.

A feeling of despair engulfed her as she saw that her would-be rescuer was not Augustus or even Carver or Jemima, but old Nanny Burtoncappe. But Nanny appeared different; less bent, more authoritative, infirmity and extreme age vanished. She wielded a great besom in her hands like a weapon, and raising it to the heavens cried, "Back, Blodeyn…back, Floralie! Break your spell! Have you not caused enough trouble for the Stannions? You flouted the rules of your own tribe and you are at fault for the consequences as much as anyone! Go back to your hill and lie quiet in the dark!"

A flash of lightning seared the heavens. A shriek and an angry wail, tailing into nothingness, sounded behind Isabella's bobbing head. The greyness faded from the lake and the churning waters deadened—reflecting once more the blue, untroubled sky of early October.

Isabella glanced up at that blessed sky, and then cold and fear claimed her and she knew no more.

"I beg you wake. Do not die. To die in such a way, would bring me more grief than you can ever imagine. I am sorry I brought you here, you do not deserve this…I am sorry."

Isabella's eyelids flickered. With a groan, she forced her eyes open and stared upwards. Through misted vision, she saw Augustus sitting on a stool beside her bed, his face a picture of distraught misery. Nanny Burtoncappe stood behind him, her grizzled old claw resting on a broad shoulder. The fierce, powerful appearance she had assumed by the lake had vanished; once more, she was a frail crone, half in her dotage, her empty gums wobbling as her mouth worked soundlessly. Her eyes, so bright at the lakeside, had returned to being hazy orbs, blue and milky with cataracts.

"How long…" Isabella managed to murmur, as she fought to sit up against the heap of frilly pillows plumped behind her.

"Days," Augustus answered. "I even had to call the doctor in, which proved greatly difficult. How could I explain to him that denizens of the Otherworld had attacked you? He thought I'd tried to murder you; I saw it in his glance. We are lucky he did not send the police to Elvingstone."

"I am thirsty," whispered Isabella. Her throat was sore and dry as dust. Nanny released Augustus's shoulder and hobbled to an ewer on the sideboard, pouring water into a glass. Carefully she held it to Isabella's parched lips.

When she had eased her thirst, Isabella stared over at Augustus, who still sat on the stool, head bowed, hands locked together. "Did you truly mean what you said, Augustus? That if I died, it would bring you grief?"

He raised his head slowly; light from the half-shuttered window streaked across his chiselled cheekbones, his firm jaw. His bright blue eyes were intense. "Yes, yes…it would. I never thought I would say such a thing; I thought I loved only her…"

"Floralie."

He nodded miserably. "I have not been honest with you, Arabella. I made a rod for my own back."

"Then be honest now. I will not think you mad. I have to believe."

Augustus took a deep breath, wincing as if in pain. "Floralie was my wife, as you know. We had a son, who died, of which you are also aware." Isabella nodded. "What I did not tell you—how could I?—was that Floralie was no ordinary woman…that she was not even a mortal woman. She came from the mound in the churchyard, and she is thousands of years old. The Elves of Elvingstone are my family's curse and their doom, you see—they were angered when my ancestor John Stannion built the first manor and have plagued us with doom and death ever since. But I thought she loved me; she even bore the words of the priest with no complaint at our wedding, but it was a front…"

Nanny cleared her throat; her senselessness had passed again and her voice was firm and lucid. "She is *Glaistig*, that is why. The Green Maiden. A snarer of men and a drinker of their blood. Did you not find that out, Augustus, my dear?"

"I did indeed." Stannion leant in Isabella's direction and with a brusque motion, pulled back the collar of his ruffled shirt. On his neck were two livid scars from puncture wounds. "That is where she drank from my veins while I slept. At first, I thought foul insects had bitten me; in summer, certain gadflies come up off the lake and are troublesome, but as time went on, I realised the truth...she drained my blood, she supped on my life-force. She did not take enough blood to kill me, but she weakened my strength greatly."

"Why did you not send her away then?" Isabella said. Her hand crept out, caught hold of Augustus' in a tight grip. Her wedding band glinted. "She may be...immortal...but surely not invulnerable? There must be ways to hold such demons at bay; surely the church could have advised?"

He bit his lower lip; it made him look younger, more vulnerable. "I was ashamed, and of course afraid that anyone I told would think me mad and have me committed. I have enemies, Arabella, and when Elvingstone's running costs led into debt, my foes gathered like an invading army, hoping to wrest it from me. If I were locked in Bedlam, raving about creatures from the Otherworld, the debtors and my opponents would ravage my estate. But of course there are other reasons I said nothing—I feared for my son, for he was born of both worlds."

"Can you bear to tell me what happened to your son?" Isabella's fingers tightened further around Augustus's in a comforting squeeze. His hand felt like a chunk of ice despite the warmth from the fire glowing in the nearby fireplace.

"Bear it, no. But tell I must. I owe it to you, Arabella. Aelfred grew up a happy lad; handsome, musical, talented. Due to the strangeness of his ancestry, he had restrictions upon his activities. Floralie had outlined what must and must not be done. Everything iron had to be removed from Elvingstone; you will note all the door handles are ceramic or brass. Horse harness was to be fitted with brass. Cutlery had to be the finest silver. Salt was forbidden on the table, and the bells in the church hung muffled and silent—the bell ringers were dismissed."

Isabella looked startled. "How did you manage that? What did the vicar say?"

"Oh, there were words between us, harsh words...but I lied and told him that my wife was an ill woman and needed rest, not to hear clashing bells. He believed me; after all, I had married her before him in the hall, at my request. She lay in a litter, wrapped in golden gauze, feigning illness—she would, of course, not stand before the altar in the church. He was not pleased by the arrangement, but I prevailed and so the wedding took place."

Augustus cleared his throat; his cheeks had lost all colour, until he appeared as pale as an alabaster effigy. "But I digress. I was to tell you about Aelfred, my poor son. Although I ceded to Floralie's wishes regarding iron in our household, I did not extend it to my collection of ancestral weapons; you have seen them, I'm sure, fastened to the top of the walls in the hall and in my dressing room and smoking room. As they were well beyond Aelfred's reach, I had no fear he would touch them…and perhaps, in my arrogance, I believed Floralie's tales about the deadliness of 'cold iron' to the Elvinkind be untrue. After all, Aelfred, was half a human child, and he favoured me in looks above his mother."

"And…it happened he got hold of one of these weapons."

"Yes. The hooks holding one sword came adrift and it fell to the floor in the hall when Floralie and I were out overseeing the planting of the gardens. Like any normal young boy, such an antique weapon fascinated him…he picked it up, and unaware of the peril, began to play with it. At eventide, we wondered where Aelfred had gone. The nurses hadn't seen him, nor had the gardeners or cook or the stable boys. We found him in the attic, rocking back and forth, back and forth, holding the lethal, fatal sword in his arms. He looked strange—not my boy at all—bloodless and withered, as if life had been drained from his limbs. Floralie began to scream; I have never heard such a heart-wrenching, awful sound, especially from one who, with her elfin ancestry, was cool and collected, even cold. She snatched Aelfred up in her arms, and the sword fell clattering from his hands—his fingers were black as if fire had scorched them."

"Oh, Augustus, what a dreadful thing to have witnessed." Isabella's own eyes filled with tears at the thought of the dying child and his distraught father.

"Floralie carried him to a couch in the drawing room and set him down. She screamed and railed at me for not removing all iron from Elvingstone. She tried to revive our son with faery kisses three, but he could not rally; he gave one little gasp, and the life passed from him. Floralie went mad; she spat the terrible truth that she had wed me only out of spite, to bring the Stannions to ruin. I asked her then why have a child that bore the name of Stannion, and she wept two ice crystal tears. She told me that her method of my ruination was to have been subtle; to have a child half-elfin holding the manor, and I, when too old and feeble to resist, taken to the elfin mound as a tithe. A tithe to hell."

Augustus took another deep breath. "She left me that day. She took Aelfred's body with her so that I could not even bury him in the church. She swore I would still, one day, pay the Elves my tithe—body and soul. I should have called for priests, exorcists…anyone for help, but I still feared they would believe me insane. And I mourned, not only for Aelfred, but also for Floralie. I loved her, despite her strangeness—perhaps because if it. Or perhaps my love was born of faery glamour and naught more. I swore I would never have truck with a female in that manner again."

Isabella wiped the corner of her eye. "If that was your oath, how did you come to ask me to be your wife? Such betrayal—I am surprised you wanted a woman here at all, even in a sham marriage."

"I lived alone, berating myself daily, for many years. Then I began noticing that colleagues began to deny me their business. My servants made inquiries and found out vile rumours had gone abroad—that I had killed my own son and that my 'missing' wife was also dead by my hand. Calls had come for me to be thoroughly investigated and sent to gaol! So much for a man being innocent until proven otherwise." His lip curled with bitter scorn. "It was then I decided that taking a new wife might deflect some of the criticism from me. If I should show myself a good husband, hopefully, men would forget the disaster of my past. But it was impossible to settle upon any lady of my station. A few were willing enough, but they were not Floralie, in face or form. One night I took myself to London to amuse myself for a few hours after a business meeting regarding repairs to the house. I hired a box in the Queen's Head Theatre. That is when I laid eyes on a beautiful young actress called Arabella Lorne."

Isabella hung her head, the coils of her hair shielding her face. "Beautiful in your eyes only because she resembled Floralie. Is that not the truth?"

Shamed, he hung his head. "Yes, I will not deny it. I treated you abominably, Arabella—like a thing, a possession. Forgive me."

With a trembling hand, she touched his wan cheek. It seemed so strange—and yet so right—to touch him, console him. "I forgive you. And I certainly do not hate you." *And what do I feel, through all this madness...*

Augustus's gaze met with hers; his soft breath flowed out, rasping between his teeth. "At one time I thought Floralie was an angel sent to me, terrible and wonderful. Now that the blinkers have fallen from my eyes, I see that you are the angel, not Floralie. And she...she was a she-devil, harsh and malevolent."

Isabella blushed and broke their gaze. "I...I am hardly an 'angel.' You don't know about me, I dare not tell you."

"I care nothing for your past; the past is buried as far as I am concerned!"

She swallowed and stared down at the coverlet. *But my 'past' is in the future, Augustus; a strange a tale as the one you've told me about your elfin wife!*

"I can't have you put at risk," Augustus continued, looking troubled. "I shall order a carriage and have you taken to safety at once."

Isabella's head shot up once more, expression fearful. "What about you, Augustus? What would you do, alone at Elvingstone?"

"Go on with my appointed fate," he said grimly, "whatever that might be. My line will no doubt end, so I no longer care. I shall be content knowing that you are safe."

Isabella sat in silence for a moment. Then she dragged herself from the bed and stood up in the frothy night-garb Nanny and Jemima had dressed her in after she was carried from the lake. Her hair tumbled over her shoulders, still caught with some weeds and grit from the deep waters. Light from the window stroked beneath her thin silks, caught highlights in her dark curls. "No, no, Augustus, I won't have it. You are not sending me anywhere. I am staying. I am, after all, your wife, even if only in name."

Augustus Stannion stared up at her, a new vulnerability evident in that austere face. The iciness of him, the coldness that had gripped his heart since the loss of Aelfred and Floralie began to melt. "You...you would do that for me, Arabella? You would stay here at Elvingstone, despite the danger?"

"Yes! Danger? I've faced lots of dangers. I cannot deny what is happening at Elvingstone confounds me, for our foes are not human beings, but I shall stand against them, and with you, in every way you can imagine. As your wife."

A silence fell. Isabella felt her head spin. She had not intended this, not at first. But if she was to be forever caught in this world of the past, she might as well snatch at happiness. And there was no one she'd ever felt such attraction for. Augustus might be dour and difficult, and harder to handle than a 'modern' man might be, but she was willing to take that chance.

"Arabella..." He rose from his stool, towering over her, taking her shoulders in his hands. The thin fabric of her nightgown crinkled; the lacing at the neckline fell away revealing smooth, creamy skin...

Nanny Burtoncappe cleared her throat noisily and averted her eyes. "I think I should go and put on the kettle! I am gasping for a good, comforting cup of tea..." she said, and she hobbled out of the door, closing it fast behind her.

"I am so glad you are staying," said Augustus, his finger tracing lightly over Isabella's parted lips. "You do not know what this means to me. It is as if a long winter has ended at Elvingstone, and the summer is ready to come in. Which is ridiculous, for it is October!"

"October it may be, but it is a time for new beginnings. We must put our old lives and old fears behind us," breathed Isabella, leaning into his embrace, thrilled and shaking with nerves at the same time. *My old life, gone forever....* A moment's dizziness gripped her, and in her mind's eye, she saw modern London, the eye of Big Ben, the racing traffic, the crowds of tourists. She saw her flat, sterile and dull, the offices she visited to pitch her work. Was she declared a missing person, another statistic? Undoubtedly, there had been a search. She'd had friends; no doubt they were stricken, even shed tears for her, held candlelit vigils and went out in search teams. But eventually their lives would go on, while the mystery of her disappearance slid away into the past...just as she had slid into the past, inhabiting the body of a dancer called Arabella Lorne...

"I...I never thought I should look upon another woman with love or desire," Augustus murmured, his voice shaking with emotion. "I thought Floralie had destroyed me. I was wrong. I was destroying myself with grief and guilt." He bent over her, tilting her head up to his. "May I kiss you, Arabella?"

"You are my husband; it is your right." She felt herself trembling. Such formal words; it that the kind of thing Victorian ladies would utter?

"I want to know you truly wish my embrace. That you do not speak kindly to me out of mere pity. If we were to be...true lovers...I cannot promise your life would be fair and fruitful... Mine is a cursed family, as I have told you."

"If there is a curse, Augustus, we will break it together!"

His mouth descended on hers, warm and gentle at first. She slid her arms around his back, revelling in sensations she had never before experienced with any man. The boyfriends of her old life…classmates, workmates, more like friends than real lovers, each one drifting away with time…

Augustus's kisses deepened, becoming more impassioned, more urgent. "Let me finally give you the wedding night we did not have, Arabella," he said huskily, hands reaching to the ribbons at the front of her gown, which had already, almost magically, started to untie. "Do not be afraid, I shall not harm you."

"I did not ever really think you would," she said. For a moment, a little fear stabbed at her—he expected her to be 'pure', but she was a twenty-six year old modern woman. However, Arabella was different, Arabella whose unscarred dancer's body was blended with her own, would be the virgin bride he expected…

The last knot was untied. Her gown fell rushing to the tiled floor. Wreathed in light from the window, she stood like a statue on a plinth in the Garden, white skin, a dancer's flat belly, pert breasts, hair falling in wild disarray like that of a pre-Raphaelite painter's model. Augustus stared at her, eyes burning with passion. Ripping off his jacket and flinging it to the ground, he lifted her in his strong arms and bore her to the bed.

Laying her out on the satin coverlet, he covered her with his own frame. Shaking, his hands explored the tempting peaks and valleys of her body. "Maybe…God willing, we can make Elvingstone thrive again," he whispered. "Maybe the world will finally come right. Maybe we can know true happiness."

"We will make it so…" she said, "the shadows of both our pasts cannot claim us!" and then she drew his head down to hers, and kissed him as passionately as he had kissed her.

Wrapped in each other's embrace, they lay entwined upon the bed, oblivious to the world about them. Oblivious to the dark crow that sat upon the exterior window moulding, watching their lovemaking through the misted glass. Its beady black eyes flared red, and behind it the sun was suddenly consumed by a cloud as dark as death.

After recovering from the shock of nearly drowning, and spending several glorious days recovering in which she did nothing but languish in Augustus's bed, Isabella arose, put on the dress of a landowner's wife, and began to work tirelessly on the arrangements for the late October ball. She made sure never to walk alone in the parkland again, however; in fact, she never went anywhere alone, even to the stables or outbuildings.

She soon learned she had been prudent in taking a companion on her travels around the estate, for a rash of unsettling events showed her that the Elves of Elvingstone were displeased at what had occurred between her and Augustus Stannion. First, the milk churns were overturned, their contents spilling all over the flagstone floor of the dairy.

Nanny Burtoncappe scanned the wreckage with her rheumy eyes. "Don't you worry, dear Miss Arabella," she soothed. "I know what to do. Jemima, get Cook Tumnel to put out some bowls of cream. A gift willingly given the Old Ones have no choice but to take, and it will sweeten their mood. Dear me, I think we have an infestation of minor fairies, brownies and boggles and the like!"

Next mishap happened in the laundry. Jemima emerged, nearly in tears, holding out one of Arabella's best dresses. Gashes ran from hem to waist and the edges looked as if tiny sharp teeth had gnawed it. "Look, it's ruined!" she cried. "Something's got to it—and I know what!"

Isabella picked up the scored green silk, making an angry noise. It had been one of her favourite gowns and now it was beyond repair. She knew the destruction had been ordered by her 'rival', Floralie. The elf-woman was sending another warning. Well, now, she had even more reasons to discard it.

Again, Nanny Burtoncappe came to the rescue. She appeared to be 'waking up' again, the torpor of age departing and her mind growing sharp. "What a shame; I'm afraid it's fit only for the bin now, Arabella. No matter, you have others as fine and dresses just aren't worth crying about; they all go out of fashion with a year anyway! However, we must make sure, though, that this unhappy little event doesn't happen again. You cannot go to the Grand Ball naked, can you now?" She tittered. "Jemima, how's your knitting going these days. Quick as you can, make the Mistress a little cap and coat. We'll leave it out on the threshold of the laundry, and when our little faerie friend shows up—a mischievous brownie, no doubt—he will take it...and vanish in a trice."

"Why should he vanish?" Isabella blinked in puzzlement. She could still scarcely believe that in a few months she had gone from a city dwelling professional, believing in only what was before her eyes, to living in a bygone era and fighting a battle on her husband's behalf against malign creatures out of a dark, unwholesome faerytale.

"Brownies come into the world naked, as do we all," said Nanny, "but they remain so without shame. There are only male brownies, you know."

"How do they…reproduce?" Despite herself, Isabella couldn't help asking. The only Brownies she knew of were twee, sweet little creatures in books she'd read at around the age of six. Or Brownies, the girl guides group.

"They don't, my dear! They burst out of acorns, fully formed. Magic acorns! But their origins aside, Brownies always regret their lack of clothes. If they are given a coat or trousers, their gratitude is so great that they vanish, never to bother the person who clothed them again."

"Then getting knitting, if you will," said Isabella, glancing towards Jemima. "I don't know if I like the idea of little, naked men lurking around the estate."

Going to the doorway of the laundry, she stared out towards the church and the haunted graveyard beyond. The yews were bending, tossing their dark heads, trees of death and the waning moon. Tumbling balls of fluff torn from an unknown, dying plant bounced and skittered on the path between them.

Nanny shuffled up to stand beside her, shading her eyes against the glare of the sky and looking in the same direction. "See those fluff-balls? Do not be fooled—more fairies. Piskies, to be exact. Don't ever follow them. You'll be pisky-led, and taken to a bad place in no time." She tapped her bristly chin with a long finger. "Now…let's see—who's free to help us? Let's get Ted the stable boy to go put salt down all around the house, keeping us separate from the church and the lands the Elves and their followers inhabit. That will keep them at bay...for a time, anyway."

The salting, knitting, and offerings of milk were soon done according to Nanny's instructions. The little suit of clothes Jemima knitted vanished; the milk bowl was licked clean. The Piskies at least seemed to have vanished. Slightly more at ease, Isabella continued to plan for the great Ball, going through the acceptance cards sent by the prospective attendees and calculating numbers, contacting musicians and deciding on music, planning what costumes she and Augustus would wear. During day, she managed the household with a skill that surprised her…and at night, she no longer stayed in her quaint, feminine bedchamber but, candle in hand, went barefoot to the master bedroom of her husband, Sir Augustus.

He would meet her with the finest wine, while on a lacquered tray beside his huge, canopied bed, four hundred years old if it was a day, lay sugared plums, selections of cheese, and mounds of imported grapes. A fire would blaze in the hearth, and he would feed her the grapes, one by one, like some decadent ancient Roman, and then they would roll in a tangle of sheets on the bed, the carvings of faces on the bedstead smiling benignly down at their passion.

Augustus's former iciness had melted forever; it seemed, at last, he had forgotten Floralie, his unearthly, unnatural first wife, in the embrace of a woman born of mortal clay. A woman beautiful but flawed, as all mortals are, but somehow the more perfect in her imperfection. A woman who chased away the dark shadows that had haunted him since the death of his only son, a victim of cold iron and faerie blood.

The day of the masked Ball grew nearer. Storms rushed in, lashing the Elvingstone estate with heavy rain, before rolling away again, leaving a cold, blue sky scored by stripped-naked tree branches that clawed like skeletal hands. A bright blood moon draped in thin rags of cloud hung between the bony boughs.

The faery hill, safe behind the protective band of salt Ted the stable hand had thrown down, lay silent and still. Augustus and Isabella climbed through the hatch in the attic roof of the manor house, bypassing poor dead Aelfric's dust-furled toys—a rocking horse, lead soldiers, a huge teddy bear with a missing eye—and stood upon the mansion's roof, gazing out at the landscaped gardens, the lake, the church…and the churchyard.

"Not a sign of movement, dearest." Augustus shaded his eyes as he observed the mound—the place where his son lay, and also the abode of the great evil that had plagued his family for generations.

"Good, I hope they stay in their malevolent realm forever." Isabella stood wrapped in a deep blue cloak, the stiff breeze blowing back her hair. There was a hard set to her jaw. Since she was now more than Augustus's wife only in name, she cared deeply for the future of the estate and the line of the Stannions—not just for her husband, though she cared for him most of all.

Augustus glanced over at Isabella and clasped her hand, gloved in fine silk, giving it a tight squeeze. "They will not give up so easily, I am certain of it, alas. I can feel a tension, an anger brewing in the air, in the earth, in the waters of the lake. Even in the flowers in our own gardens. Can you not feel it, sweetling?"

Uneasily Isabella leant on the parapet of the manor. Before her, stretched the gardens, the topiary hedges, the rosary with the metal sundial, the lake with its shaded ring of trees and stones and the broken fountain in the centre. "I want to deny it, but I fear I can. I had prayed it was merely my imagination because the Ball is now so near and I want it all to go right. To be safe for us and for our guests."

Nervously, she began to twist a coil of hair around her hand. There were things she could not tell him. Last night and the night before, she'd dreamed of London. Modern London. They were lucid dreams—she smelt the streets, the car exhaust, the scent of food from various restaurants. She was running down the lane leading from the Queen's Head, out towards her car, towards her old life. Yet, she wasn't happy in the dream; she was crying bitterly… Was someone or something drawing her back to her own time? She didn't know…nor did she know how to stop it.

"The Otherworlders will do something evil at the Ball, I feel it in my heart of hearts." Augustus' brow creasing with a frown. "Floralie will never let me go so easily. The Elves of Elvingstone are dark and devious beings."

"We still have one more day to prepare," said Isabella, turning to him and slipping into his embrace as the wind in that high place buffeted them both. He felt solid and real; more so than her memories of the 21st century. "I will ask Nanny's advice."

Nanny Burtoncappe was up and about the mansion, striding through the hallways giving orders to a host of hired staff helping prepare for the Ball. Once again, there seemed no sign of frailty in the ancient woman; her eyes had lost their milky hue and she stood upright without any aid in her wide-brimmed bonnet and antique crinoline.

"Nanny, I must speak with you." Isabella swept towards her with an unsmiling face.

Nanny gazed shrewdly at her mistress, then nodded. Taking Isabella by the elbow, she led her into an alcove near the fireplace in the Great Hall, well out of earshot of the hired help. Servants swirled throughout the room, dusting and polishing, laying out tables, bringing out trays of glasses and cutlery. "What is it, my dear Arabella? Are you and the Master well? You look upset."

"We are both very well...but I cannot deny it, we are afraid of...*them*. We can sense malice all around us; evil rising to take revenge. I...I don't know why, but I think you might be the only one who has the knowledge of how we might protect ourselves."

"Well might you and the Master be afraid." Nanny sombrely pursed her thin, dry lips. The expression made her small face break into a thousand lines, like a shattered mirror. "The Fae do not have the mores of mortal men and their hatreds can last for eternity. Capricious, beautiful...and deadly."

"What are they, Nanny?" Isabella asked plaintively.

"There are many theories, my dear. I do not know which is true, and I believe they do know the truth of their origins either. Some say they are the spirits of the ancient dead, one-time guardians of the land we live in; others claim they are fallen angels, too wicked for heaven, too good for hell."

"I think they deserve to burn in hell, if such a place exists!" Isabella cried, crossing her arms defensively. "What they have done to Augustus and his family is dreadful. And...and they tried to murder me, when I had never done anything to them."

"I understand how bitter the Master must feel. I do not condone the Elves' actions, but believe it or not, Mistress Bella, I feel some compassion for the Elder Folk. Imagine what it is like for them; living centuries while the world they knew withers and changes, gone forever. The land of untouched hills, valleys, and mountains that once ruled is gone. Mortal men have inherited the earth. Now we live in an age where gas lamps may light the darkest night. The stars have grown dim. Smoke stacks blight green fields and red brick sprawls over one-time Elfin territories. The Old Ones have been pushed aside, thrust into the dark, lonely corners of the world like the mound in Elvingstone's churchyard. No wonder they are angry and vengeful—they, who lived like gods not so long ago!"

Isabella shivered. "I still feel no pity. If I could have but one wish, it would be that they left Elvingstone forever. And if that is impossible, at least for the Ball to be safe for our guests. Can you help us in that regard, Nanny? You seem to have great knowledge of these otherworldly matters."

She stared down the dwarfish form of the old woman, marvelling. How could she have thought Nanny senile and incapable when she first arrived at Elvingstone? Yet so she had seemed, rocking back and forth and singing her dark ditties. It was as if a spell had been lifted from her, revealing the true Nanny—old yet filled with unseen strength.

Nanny rubbed her chin and narrowed her eyes, deep in thought. "I will do my best, Mistress. Stronger wards must be set. I will send for the village smith. Horseshoes."

"Pardon me?" Isabella frowned, not sure if she misheard. "Did I hear you rightly, Nanny? Horseshoes?"

"Yes, my dear, horseshoes. There are two reasons they may help. They are made of iron, for one, deadly to the Old Ones, but they are also symbols of good luck tied to the Moon. Trust me, my dear. I will also have Jemima give some more offerings to the Elves; it may keep them quieter than they would be otherwise, although there is no guarantee that will be the case. They become more excitable around the Feast of All Hallows, for the veils between worlds grow thin at that time. Hmm now, I wonder where Jemima had got to? I haven't seen her all day."

"I believe she is helping Cook Tumnel in the kitchen."

"I will go and find her, and advise what must be done before the Ball."

"I shall come with you, Nanny."

They found Jemima, as expected, in the confines of the ancient kitchen, with its greasy, heat-crackled tiling and workaday brick floor. Scores of battered copper pots and pans hung from hooks on the walls, and from the wooden beams overhead dangled handfuls of herbs wrapped in bright ribbons, which sent off a pungent scent that mingled with pervasive cooking smells.

Cook was thrusting a tray into the roaring oven, while Jemima laboured upon a long wooden table, its surface scored by centuries of knife cuts. She was kneading dough, her arms covered in white flour almost up to the elbow.

"Jemima, we have need of you," said Nanny. "My old legs won't carry me down to the village. We need a dozen horseshoes, the very best the smith can make. Once you have them, we need them laid out at intervals around the site of the Master's Ball. The arms of the horseshoe must face outwards, away from Elvingstone—do you understand?"

Jemima ceased kneading the dough and wiped her hands on her grubby apron. She nodded. "Yes, Nanny. A dozen horseshoes, ordered this afternoon, and when delivered by Smith Tooker, laid out around the garden where the Ball will take place. Near the salt circle, with the arms facing out towards Elvingstone's perimeter fence."

"Correct. We also need the…offering. The 'wine.' The sweet red wine the Elfinkind desire. Can you do that as well for me, Jemima? Bless you, child, for being this old woman's hands and legs."

"Of course I can do it, Nanny." Jemima pushed the mixing bowl aside, still showering white flour. "In fact, I'll get the offering now, shall I? Get started on what needs to be done. The sooner the better, then there will be no mad rush."

Turning on her heel, the maid grabbed something off the sideboard and ran out through the kitchen door into the yard. A flurry of feathers and raucous, annoyed squawking filled the air; Cook kept chickens and pheasants in several long runs outside, ready for the pot.

Suddenly the angry squawks became terrified screeching that was abruptly cut short.

"What on earth?" cried Isabella, hand pressed to her heart in alarm. "It sounds as if she's kil…"

Grinning with satisfaction, Jemima appeared in the doorway. Blood smeared her face in stripes; contrasted with the dusting of flour, it looked as though she was wearing primitive war-paint. In her hand, she gripped a headless chicken's body, still struggling in a horrible mockery of life.

She flung the corpse into a shallow bowl held out by Cook, and Isabella watched in horror as blood bubbled up to the white porcelain rim. As the bowl filled, Jemima took a kitchen knife and pricked her own palm. Droplets of red dropped down to mingle with the steaming chicken blood.

"This should keep the Elves of Elvingstone happy," said Jemima, sounding pleased with herself, as she stirred the bowl with a ladle. "Fresh. Sweet. Partly human."

Isabella's head swam as the iron taint of blood struck her nostrils. "I…I did not think you meant that kind of …more blood. Does this really help? Or does it just encourage them to come back for more?"

Bile rising into her mouth, she turned and rushed out of the kitchen, slamming the door on both Nanny and Jemima. She glanced down as she fled along the hall; her pale gold skirts were speckled with blood drops, clinging to the silk like tiny red rubies. Just like her wedding dress when her husband had poured Otis Hubbard's blood before the rusty doors of the Stannion crypt.

Whose blood would next be spilled for the Elves of Elvingstone?

Would it be her own?

Dusk descended over Elvingstone Manor, a blue shroud punctuated by the wavering light of torches placed at even intervals around the estate's gardens. The lake was a sheet of rippling golden flame, the banks decorated with glowing paper lanterns. Violinists played upon a small barge at the centre, dressed in costumes from centuries past—powdered periwigs and gold brocade suits. The house itself had two fire barrels blazing upon the parapet, attended by hired servants bearing water-buckets should anything go amiss. Below, the front door gaped wide in welcome, emitting a hazy stream of light that fanned out across the drive.

Inside the manor, a stream of guests in outlandish costumes sipped sherry from crystal glasses in the Hall of Mirrors. Fat old lords from the city, former colleagues of Augustus' father, reclined on the thrones set between each looking- glass, tipsy even at the early hour, all fancying themselves as little kings. Their wives trotted around with powdered faces and domes of starched hair, waving decorated fans in front of their painted faces as they gossiped. Locals were there too, standing apart from the wealthier classes in simple but often vaguely disturbing costumes of witches, warlocks and ghosts. Never did the two groups converse, and the City ladies seemed scandalised that they should share the room with the working class. However, it was Augustus Stannion's Ball, and attendees had always included rich and poor.

In the main hall, a trestle table stood covered with a starched white cloth. Silver platters held an array of marvellous and unusual dishes—marbled veal, pheasant pie, chickpeas strewn with asparagus spears, stewed cardoons, roast hares swimming in Pompadour cream, and a sweet, sugary jelly covered in a silvered web.

Folk of both high and low estate clustered round the table, while servants ladled the fare onto antique china platters decorated with the Stannion family crest. Violinists careered around the feasters, while a masked baritone sang from a podium near the fireplace.

"Is everything going as it should, do you think, Augustus?" Dressed as the embodiment of coming Winter, with a white face-mask, a tiara with gems patterned into snowflakes, and crystal 'icicles' fastened to a silver gown, Isabella pulled her husband into a corner

Augustus wore the costume of a highwayman from bygone centuries, complete with bicorn hat and long riding boots up to the thigh. "I am still uneasy, dear heart, but perhaps that is to be expected. Did you yourself not inform me that wards have been set to help keep us safe?"

"Yes, the horseshoes…and the offering." Isabella made a face. "Oh Augustus, how I hate that part of it, most of all. Blood…No good can come of it."

"Do not speak of it then." Augustus grasped her hand in his black-gloved one and raised it to his lips. "Let us not think overmuch of the accursed Elves and their hatred for us…while still remaining aware of potential dangers, of course. The Ball is meant to be a joyous occasion, and its renewal not only revived an old tradition, but hopefully my fortunes too. Already here is good news in that regard, my dearest."

"What news? What has happened?" Isabella tugged at his cravat playfully. "We could use some good news!"

"As you are undoubtedly aware, the manor house is crumbling away around us. My finances are as ruinous as Elvingstone. For years I had resented holding the October Ball because I knew it would near enough bankrupt me every time. My neighbours and acquaintances ate my food and drank my claret while the bloody roof needed new tiles and woodworms gnawed the panels in the great hall. But…it seems one of my mother's uncles, an old bachelor of remote age, has recently died and left me a legacy in his will. On top of that, in the past few days, I have managed to sell some lands owned by the family that are redundant for my purposes. I made a greater sum than anticipated. Arabella Lorne, my dearest wife, I believe you have brought me much-needed good luck."

"And I hope I shall continue to do so, Augustus." She blushed suddenly, hectically behind her mask.

He gazed down at her, his eyes burning through the slits in his black highwayman's mask. "Now all we need is an heir for the estate. Not just one child but a whole house full of them, the boys carrying on the Stannion name and the girls as fair and talented as their mother."

Isabella tried to grin. She had not really thought of children, but of course, in a pre-birth control world it was highly likely…She just hoped she would not end up with ten or more! Or die in childbirth like so many women of the day… "We will just have to see what time brings, won't we?"

"If we were indeed so blessed as to have children, then I would truly believe the curse had been lifted from my family." He hung his head and for a moment, Isabella thought he would weep—her tall, imposing husband who had at one time seemed so icy, so untouchable…but who was full of untouched passions beneath the glacial surface "Now, come with me, my dearest; let us dance the night away in celebration! Let us put our troubles behind us!"

Arm around Isabella's waist, Augustus whisked her out of the great hall and raced her down the Hall of Mirrors, where their costumed images multiplied and ran alongside them, warped to deformity by the bends in the dim old glass. Out of the front door they raced, laughing, past the sundial in the rosery and the little ornamental fountain in the Italian Garden where, for this night only, red wine spewed from the mouths of carved cherubs round the rim into the waiting goblets of the partygoers.

Reaching Elvingstone's vast topiary garden, the couple passed through hedges fashioned into domes and towers, cats, cockerels and peacocks, until they reached the lantern-lit path leading to the Paladin's Bower, where the night's dancing was scheduled to take place below the moon and stars. Scores of revellers followed them, a flowing tide of men, women and children in strange disguises—cutlass wielding pirates, haloed angels, birds with jewelled beaks, white-sheeted ghosts, a whimsical donkey, and a plethora of bygone kings, queens and princesses in crowns or conical hats and trailing cloaks of royal purple.

Paladin's Bower was a stretch of neatly-cropped green lawn flanked by Rhododendron bushes grown to a great height. The bushes bore no flowers, for it was not the season; instead, hundreds of paper lanterns with candles fluttering inside dangled from every branch. Paste jewels glimmered on chains next to the lanterns, reflecting their tentative light.

At the end of the lawn stood a small, stone summerhouse with an oriental appearance: a roof that curved upwards at the corners and large round windows covered by crisscrossed lead inlay. The largest window of all emitted rich, golden light; it opened up onto a balcony with gilded railings all around. A small troupe of musicians sat on chairs on the lawn before the summerhouse; as Isabella and Augustus approached laughing and imbibing wine as they walked, they began to play a haunting, romantic air. Isabella was reminded of the piece by Saint-Saens known as '*Danse Macabre*'…but that score would not be written till the 1870's.

Isabella had frequently explored the Elvingstone estate but had never entered the summerhouse in the Paladin's Bower. Augustus had never offered the key to the interior and she had never asked. She assumed it was ruinous like the fountain in the lake and that he was ashamed for her to see inside.

As she drew near, she noted the rounded arches of the windows, pock-marked with age, the fabric poorly maintained—they bore the heraldic designs and mottoes so beloved of Augustus's father and grandfather. Faded blue and red chevrons decorated the stonework; *I won my spurs upon my King's Crusade* was written in fancy gold script around the window's rim.

Pulling away from her husband, Isabella mounted the first stair leading to the doorway. Over the curved roofline, the moon beamed down, hooked, deep in its waning phase—a lean, sinister Old Man with dark, skull eye-hollows. She shivered suddenly, and it was not from the chill of the evening. A tang of sulphur hung in the air, possibly from the fireworks that were stored nearby for a brief display at the end of the evening; but there was also a cold green smell—earth, dankness, graveyard mould.

"Arabella, dear wife, you do not want to go in there." Augustus reached out to catch her elbow, preventing her from ascending the rest of the steps.

"Why ever not, Augustus?" She turned to face her husband; to her dismay, she noticed that his old, shuttered, secretive expression had returned. "Surely, as your wife, there is no part of the Elvingstone estate I cannot visit."

His face contorted, assuming a smile she immediately recognised as false. "There's no time, my darling. Our guests want to see us dance, my dear. As patrons of the Ball, it is our duty to join in, to take the lead, to get everyone enjoying themselves. Many of our guests have heard of your dancing skills and are eager to see you perform. Come…" He stretched out his hand to catch hers; his grip was firm, brooking no argument.

She dared not say no, but, biting her lip, let him lead her out onto the lawns of the Paladin's Bower. The waiting musicians struck up a livelier tune, which they played with gusto while the guests crowded in, sweeping over the green grass carpet in their fabulous costumes—a mixture of crowns and veils and cloaks, Papier Mache animal heads and glittering paste jewels.

Isabella danced with Augustus, as the occasion demanded, and for a time her uneasiness fled as she gazed into his riveting blue eyes. The fear of the Elves of Elvingstone abated; she thought only of the magic of the night and the unexpected love for the man with whom she danced. The man of her great great great grandparents' generation…

The dancers were swaying around them now, losing their rhythm as alcohol and high spirits obliterated the stateliness of the initial minuets, gavottes and sarabandes. Laughing, intoxicated people began to crash into each other; ladies shrieked, their hems trodden on and torn, while lines of dancers careered off the lawn and stumbled into the bare Rhododendron bushes.

At the same time, a freezing wind began to blow, rising from nowhere with a howl like a soul in torment. Hats were knocked off and outside the dancing area, a table filled with wine glasses overturned with a crash. Ladies' shawls whipped through the air, and lanterns torn from the Rhododendron bushes went sailing into the sky, showering glitter in their wake.

Isabella staggered as the unnatural wind hit her; it felt as if fists pummelled her flesh, seeking to strike her down. Augustus clung grimly to her shoulders, as his bicorn hat flew off and vanished somewhere in the darkness.

All laughter ceased and the revellers began to panic, running this way and that in dismay. "Hold! It is only a sudden gust of wind!" Augustus roared, but the partygoers would not be calmed.

Out of the mayhem, a dwarfish male figure appeared. It careered towards Isabella and Augustus, running fast as if driven by the wind. Isabella noticed a silverish, scaly body, immodestly dressed in a loincloth, and a broad pumpkin-head with pointed ears tufted with fur. The creature carried a jar tied to a long stick; the jar, swaying in the gale, was filled with what seemed to be bees or wasps, dipping and dashing at the glass.

"Watch out, man!" Augustus shouted angrily as the manikin appeared to stumble and the jar on its pole toppled towards the ground. "Have a care!"

Isabella flung up her arm to shield herself. The pole struck the ground and the jar shattered, sending fragments of glass spiralling into the air. Buzzing angrily, the insects imprisoned within flew out and darted at Isabella and Augustus, whirling around their heads in a crown of phosphorescence.

"Oh!" Isabella clutched at her shoulder. "One of them has stung me! It burns…it burns, but not like fire, like ice!"

Augustus roared in outrage and pursued the dwarfish little man across the lawn. The creature was hopping on one broad foot and laughing. "Who the hell are you? What have you done?"

The little man thrust out a forked tongue. "I am Lob-Lie-By-The-Fire; I serve as Lady Blodeyn's squire! I nip and dip between the trees, bringing with me Elfin bees, fierce hornets and the Dumbledore…to plague you humans evermore!"

Augustus let out another infuriated bellow and dived for the manikin. The dwarf spat in his direction, then wriggled under the knotted roots of one of the Rhododendrons and vanished from view. Hands clenching and unclenching in anger, Augustus whirled away from the site of his disappearance and stormed back to Isabella.

"I don't feel well, Augustus." Isabella pulled off her mask. She had gone grey; beads of icy sweat stood out on her forehead.

"God help us, it's the Old Ones!" Augustus spat. "They have crept into the main grounds somehow; they have either overcome the wards or we've been betrayed by someone we trusted. I won't let them take you, Isabella; they won't rob me of my wife" I'll get you indoors, out of harm's way, and summon the doctor from the village."

Lifting her in his arms, he carried her towards the summerhouse. The lanterns had gone out in the windows, extinguished by the unnatural wind, and all was in darkness. Cursing, he shifted Isabella to his shoulder and fumbled in his belt-pouch for the key that would unlock the brass bound door.

"I thought you didn't want me to go inside," she whispered against the dark fabric of his costume. Her head spun; her lips felt numb, tingling. Above her in the sky, the moon's face contorted, became an evil, fanged visage that spat down its malice in the form of cold bluish light.

"I didn't and still don't, but not because it can bring any harm to you. It is because of my own folly, which is on display inside. I am ashamed, Arabella. You will see why."

He bore her into a narrow corridor; a single lantern had stayed alight here, casting a pallid glow onto walls dark and sweating, with moss growing between the masonry joints. Remnants of gold painted heraldic shields gleamed out, and the eggshell-blue ceiling ceiling, where damp had not patched it, was dotted with thin-pointed gilt stars. At the far end of the corridor slumped a rusty suit of armour on a stand.

Isabella almost expected the armour to come to life and clatter menacingly towards her, animated by some creature out of the faery hill but, mercifully, it remained motionless.

Augustus carried her to another staircase and climbed. After a few minutes of stumbling in the dark, they entered the penultimate chamber, with the balcony overlooking the grass dancing area. "Can you stand?" asked Augustus. "If you can, I will relight the lamps."

Isabella was not at all sure; her head was whirling, her eyesight fading in and out, her shoulder burning with cold fire where the Elfin insect had attacked her. Nonetheless, she said, "Yes, I can stand. We must have light. I would rather face *them* in light than the shadows."

Gently Augustus set her down. She leaned against the wall, weak and faint, as he fiddled with several oil lamps. A moment later they kindled, casting a warm glow on walls hung with moth-eaten tapestries that depicted medieval scenes of the hunt. A chaise longue cushioned in red and gold stood in the corner amidst a hodgepodge of antique furniture: ivory elephants holding up jade planters, teak wood dressers inlaid with abalone shell.

But Isabella did not look at this faded luxury. It meant nothing to her, mostly rather garish Victoriana.

Instead, her eyes were drawn to the centre of the chamber, and her hand went to her mouth to stifle a horrified gasp.

At the heart of the room, under a crack-lined plaster dome, stood an immense, lavish, and gaudy statue carved from alabaster. It was of Augustus...and his first wife, Floralie. Augustus was on his knees, degraded, worshipful, weak before the radiant, goddess-like form of Floralie. Floralie, looking so much like Isabella/Arabella they could almost have been twins, save for the cruel, mocking smile that lifted her lips.

"I told you my shame was hidden in here," said Augustus roughly. He reached out and lifted Isabella again, placing her down upon the chaise longue and brushing back her hair from her damp forehead. "I promise I will get rid of it. I will have workmen come with hammers tomorrow and shatter the ugly thing into pieces! I should have done so long ago!"

"Augustus, Augustus, it does not matter, it's only a statue." Isabella arched her back against the cushions on the chaise longue. "Ah, I wish I knew what was happening to me. Such a little nip...but I feel so cold, so strange. I've never reacted badly to a bee sting before...but that probably wasn't a normal bee."

Augustus ran his thumb over the tiny red pinprick on her arm. "Your skin...it is as cold as ice. I am sending everyone home, sending for the doctor."

Tears pooled in Isabella's eyes. "But can any human doctor heal me? Would they even believe it if we told them? Augustus, I am so afraid...."

"I won't lose you!" Augustus teeth were gritted; he looked a madman, his eyes shining, glassy. "Not when I have found you, and at long last, my sins are expiated and my luck returned!"

"Maybe it hasn't returned!" Isabella closed her eyes and lay back on the chaise longue, as her ears buzzed and black spots clouded her vision. "Maybe we were deceived. Augustus, forgive me, I am so sorry..."

Suddenly there was a clattering on the stone steps outside the chamber door. Isabella managed to raise herself on a shaking elbow as Nanny Burtoncappe sailed into the room, the folds of her voluminous black cloak billowing behind her like vast wings.

"Nanny!" Isabella and Augustus cried out, almost in unison.

"I have come, my dears!" Nanny pushed past Augustus and rushed to Isabella's side, feeling her pulse with her bony fingers and wiping her brow with a handkerchief. "My dear, you must be honest with me. I don't need you to tell me how you feel, but I must know, what can you *see*?"

Isabella rubbed her eyes with her knuckles. "Black dots, whirring like bees pouring from a disturbed hive, but they are not bees." She gazed up towards the ceiling, fearful yet awestruck. "I can see winged beings flying, tiny figures with swords made of rose-thorns. And their faces...ghosts, pale and beautiful but menacing. They hold out their hands to me and beckon, crying, *Come to us, come down into the dark earth under hill.*"

"They are not ghosts," said Nanny sharply. "Merely minions of the Elves, wicked lesser beings under their thrall. The poison they have given you is an attempt to drag your soul into their realm."

Augustus made a sputtering sound. "Isabella is a God-fearing woman; they cannot have her soul. Or her body. Nanny…" He grasped the older woman's thin shoulders, his knuckles bone-white. "Nanny, you have served my family time out of mind. You stood in as my mother when my own mother died. Your wisdom has helped me to survive at Elvingstone, to keep my very sanity. If you can do just one more thing for me, let it be this…save my new wife. Save Arabella from those foul demons from the churchyard!"

"It is fully my intention to, Augustus," Nanny said crisply. "Arabella, look at me, my girl…you must tell me, where did they place their mark on you?"

Fingers numb and shaking, Isabella rolled back her sleeve. A little purple bruise marred the flesh of her upper arm. "A glowing…fly or wasp…it either bit or stung me."

Nanny prodded the livid spot with a finger. "Not an insect, my poor dear. A small sprite attacked you, one of the winged beings you can see flying in the air. I know what they've used as a weapon, the wicked creatures. A minute faery thorn, dipped in gall, has burrowed its way in and makes its inexorable journey towards the heart."

"Can you get it out?" asked Augustus. "God Almighty, please tell me that you can."

"I will try my best." Nanny's lips drew tightly together. "But you must stop your bellowing, Augustus! It is too distracting. You sound just as you did when you were a little lad and no one paid you attention. I would advise you go and make yourself useful elsewhere on the estate; your guests are terrified and the Fae are abroad. Like the birthing chamber, what must take place in this room tonight is not fit for the eyes of anxious husbands."

Augustus sprang back as if he had been struck. His face grew as hard as granite. "Yes, yes, I will make myself useful. I will do what I should have done years ago! I will finish it for once and for all!" Reaching under his highwayman's cloak, he pulled out an old-fashioned pistol. It was no toy, no stage prop for the costume ball, but a real weapon capable of firing.

Nanny stared at her former charge, eyes narrowed. "What on earth are you intending to do with that gun, Augustus? You know the Elves are immortal; they cannot be killed by mortal means. Yes, yes, strike them with sword or bullet and they will fall down and bleed green blood like tree-sap, but within a few months they return, like weeds returning to choke the garden."

A bitter, tight smile pulled Augustus's lips back in a mirthless grin. "I am aware of that, Nanny; I was fooled once but I am no one's fool now. There is one thing the Elves hate. One thing they cannot abide. The very thing that killed my only son. Iron. They fear it, and it is the one thing that is lethal to them. I have held discourse with a smith as to my needs, and hence my pistol is loaded with bullets fashioned from iron."

"Augustus, be careful if you intend to follow this course!" Nanny held up her hand in warning. "With iron bullets, you may be successful in killing Elves, but the Old Ones are stronger than any human and tricksy. What use your gun and special bullets, if you are sung into a stupor by some siren, or struck by elf-shot from a faery bow?"

"Nanny, be silent; I will not be stopped. As I said before, I will make an end to this madness. Do not worry about me, Nanny—tend to my wife instead! She needs you more than I!"

Pistol in hand, Augustus clattered down the stairs of the summerhouse, while Nanny turned back to Isabella. Reaching to a purse attached to her belt, she pulled out a little knife. Isabella jumped at the sight of its sharpened blade gleaming dully in the wavering light. "Nanny, do you always carry such a weapon?"

"Yes, Yes, I do," said the ancient woman, testing the blade between finger and thumb. "It can be useful for protection...or for more practical purposes. Now, child, are you going to be brave?"

"I will try! What choice do I have?" She swallowed, thinking of the chances of fatal infection in this pre-anti-biotic world.

"Take that pillow you are lying against and bite down upon it when the pain is at its worst. I must dig that lethal thorn out of your flesh as soon as possible."

Isabella looked horrified, but she pressed the pillow to her face and held out her arm. Livid blue streaks now radiated out from the small hole where the faery thorn had entered. Mere seconds before, they had not existed. The poison, ice-cold and deadly, was spreading.

Face solemn, Nanny poked the wound again with long, prying fingers. "It's on the move, the accursed thing, but I have located it. Now, dear, it is time for you to be brave—no more procrastination. This procedure will be deeply unpleasant...but necessary."

With the practised manner of a nurse, Nanny Burtoncappe tied a tourniquet around the top of Isabella's arm. "Forgive me for making it so tight, but it is to help control the poison's spread."

The knot tied, she pressed the tip of her knife into Isabella's flesh. The girl gasped aloud then pressed the pillow to her mouth to stifle any outcry. Tears of pain trickled from the corners of her eyes as blood rushed down her arm and dripped like red blossoms onto the polished tiles of the summerhouse.

"Damn them, damn them!" Nanny murmured as she prodded with her blade. Beads of sweat jewelled her brow and dangled from the tip of her pointed nose. "It has gone deep, so deep..."

Suddenly a triumphant grin spread across her aged features. "Aha, success at last! I've found the evil little thing!"

Nanny made a flicking motion with her knife. A small object, showering blood, cartwheeled through the air and fell to the floor with a tinkling noise. Hook-shaped and coloured pale blue, it looked almost like a piece of glass or chip of ice. Coldness radiated from it; in the room, the lamps hissed and sank low, verging on dying, while frost filled the panes of glass in the leaded windows.

"Accursed sorcery!" Eyes blazing, Nanny stepped on the faery thorn with the heel of her shoe and ground it to nothingness on the tiles.

Instantly, the frosting of ice melted in the window. The lamps roared to golden life and the temperature shot back to normal. Isabella sat up, the pillow she'd bitten in her agony now pressed against the wound in her arm. Colour rushed back into her cheeks and lips.

"Nanny, Nanny, thank goodness you came to the Bower! The normal world is returning. The faery people have vanished; my limbs are no longer weak and my vision is clear! I feel perfectly well, as if nothing had happened! It's nothing short of a miracle… I must find Augustus and tell him…."

"No," admonished Nanny Burtoncappe, catching Isabella's arm. "For all that you feel better now, you were in grave danger, more than you realised. Stay and rest a while; you are safer in the summerhouse than outside."

"But he may be harmed, facing those monsters on his own! I can't leave him out there alone! You don't understand!"

"Of course I understand, Arabella. I have loved him like a son from the moment he was born. He was my charge and my delight. I cared for him, taught him, scolded him when he misbehaved. Only I could get him to obey; even his father had no control over his actions. Augustus would listen only to me; listen, even if he did not always act on my advice. As when he married that unnatural creature, Floralie…."

At that moment, another violent gust of wind struck the summerhouse. The windowpanes rattled, the doors banged. The lamps dimmed again, reduced to red embers, and a rat-tat-tat noise, like a dog's nails on a hard floor, sounded across the dome of the roof.

"What on earth is that?" Isabella leapt from the chaise longue, staring up at the ceiling. The skittering was now replaced by a clawing sound, as if talons were dug into the fabric of the roof, seeking to rend the decayed stonework apart. A ringing, as of tiny crystal bells, filled the air, the sound sinister rather than beautiful.

Gazing up, Nanny's lips quivered. "They try to bind me with Fae music from the Silver Apple Branch!" she gasped. "Curse them…it is strong…too strong…" she staggered back and suddenly her face sagged, slumped, the creases pouring down like candle wax.

"Nanny!" screamed Isabella, fearing the old woman was having a seizure of a stroke. She wondered if she could remember any first aid…

Nanny Burtoncappe slumped to the floor, head lolling forward. "He is coming…the King…the White King…" she murmured, eyes rolling back in her head until only the white showed. "The wards have been completely shattered, the tribute taken but denied. We are undone." A trail of drool, slug-thick, dangled from the corner of her mouth, her limbs hung akimbo like those of a rag doll.

Isabella clawed at her shoulder, trying to rouse her, dragging her into a sitting position. Nanny's head flopped back and forth, back and forth on its skinny neck. The wise, helpful Nanny Burtoncappe had vanished completely and the old crone that Isabella first met at Elvingstone came to the fore once again—blear-eyed and cataract-ridden, half-living in another world. Nanny began to rock and chuckle, as more drool hit the front of her dress.

In a slurred voice, she sang a dreary carol from northern England,, where men carried coffined corpses on Lych-walks between the lonely villages of moorland and upland:

"This Fae night, this Fae night,
Every night and all,
Fire and sleet and candlelight—
May Christ receive thy soul!"

"Oh, Nanny…" As the old woman's head lolled limply forward again, Isabella let her slide onto the tiles then clambered unsteadily to her feet. She could do no more to assist. Cutting a strip from her skirts using Nanny's knife, she bound it around her wounded arm and raced down the stairs towards the door. She had no idea what was perched upon the summerhouse's roof, but she dared not stay inside, a prisoner with a gibbering, mad or enchanted old crone.

Reaching the lowest step, she was reaching for the handle of the outer door when she heard a voice shouting in the darkness beyond. A man's voice, raised in wrath. *Augustus!*

Abruptly the shouting ceased, and there were three loud bangs—the noise of a pistol firing repeatedly—followed by a strangled yells, harsh with rage and despair, and the sound of people screaming in terror.

"Augustus!" cried Isabella in alarm, and she burst from the summerhouse, and hoisting up her ruined gown sprinted across the lawns of the Paladin's Bower.

Outside, the world she knew had changed. The party lanterns had burnt out or fallen, but an eerie light that had no source illuminated the greensward. The wild, supernatural winds had torn away all the decorations for the Ball, but the great, bare Rhododendron bushes were now wreathed in deep, bluish phosphorescence as flowers born of wildfire and witchlight opened rotting petals that emitted a charnel reek, a mixture of sweetness and the rankness of fleshly decay.

Flinging her arm across her nose to cut the vile scent, Isabella fled across the grass. Beneath her shoes, the dew had frozen into crystals; grass stems bent and snapped.

As the trees surrounding Paladin's Bower fell away, she gazed across the rest of the gardens toward the dark block of the manor house. Faintly she could see figures flying down the drive towards the gates, crashing through the woods in terrified panic—the guests escaping from what they could not understand, from an old, half-forgotten myth that had become a horrible reality. The bushes in the maze were standing like children's tops, frozen; the rosery wine-fountain glittering with icicles; the surface of the lake glimmered under a sheet of thin ice. Balls of incandescence rolled along the crenellated rooftop of Elvingstone manor, while the westering moon sank into a red veil of clouds, the cruel, coy Man in the Moon peering through a faint veil of blood.

"Augustus!" she cried, her voice ringing out into the haunted night. "Augustus, where are you? Please, God, please, let him be unhurt..." A sob tore at her throat and her neck muscles spasmed painfully. She fought the urge to weep, to become hysterical. She felt so alone. Nanny was no help now and might never be again, for all Isabella knew; the guests and servants had fled, and Augustus was nowhere in sight. Perhaps he was injured...perhaps he was dead. The remembered sound of his pistol firing rang incessantly through her brain.

In the gloom of the bushes behind her, branches rustled, silkily, stealthily. There was a jingle, jingle sound; ice bells, sinister and surreal. The death-scent that clung to the Rhododendron forest lifted; suddenly Elvingstone's gardens were filled with the aroma of blooming spring flowers—lily-of-the-valley, hyacinth, daffodil, orchids and bluebells.

Isabella felt her spine tingle. She would not, could not, bear to glance over her shoulder. She knew someone, some *THING* was behind her, and feared to face whatever creature approached through the glowing foliage.

As she stood, poised for flight, terror knotting her innards, a great white wolf padded out of the murk and squatted on its haunches before her. Blue-eyed, red-eared, it wore a collar studded with crystal spikes as sharp as blades. A scarlet tongue rolled over damp, glittering fangs. The beast observed her hungrily and skulked in her direction, mouth fixed in a canine grin.

Isabella cried out and leapt away from the wolf, seeking mindlessly for a tree branch—*anything* she might use as a weapon against the unearthly predator.

As she did, a hand descended on her shoulder. "Face me, Isabella Lawrence." Cold breath froze the shell of her ear. The voice was male, unfamiliar, and weirdly accented, almost mechanical and stilted, as if emerging from lips that seldom used human speech.

She did not want to turn, to see the one with the frigid breath, the deadly voice, the hand that rested oh-so-lightly and yet menacingly on her shoulder. The creature that knew her true name, although they had never met...

But she was turning, her ankles bending against her will, her whole body jerking around as if she were a marionette with its strings being yanked and pulled this way and that by a petulant child. Beside her, the blue-eyed wolf in its sparkling collar threw up its snout towards the blood-tinged rind of the moon and released a yammering howl of victory.

Isabella tried to screw her eyes shut, still unwilling to gaze upon whatever held her fast in its spell, but even such simpler defiance was denied her—her head was tilted backwards, and her eyelids forced rigidly open as if they were pinned in place.

A tall man stood upon the shimmering ice-lawn. No, not a man, not a mortal man, at least. An Elfin male, one of the Fae of legend, both beautiful and sinister at once. As tall as a sapling, a pallid light glowed within his breast as if he were a living lantern; it spilled down through his torso and his limbs, lighting up traceries of veins that pumped no human blood. Snow-hued hair, tinged by the blue of winter shadows, streamed over his shoulders and down his back, coiling and writhing. Golden hair tresses of ancient design clung to the ends, rattling together like the bones of disturbed skeletons—and indeed, around his swan-graceful neck dangled a necklace of blue faïence and strung bones—human knuckles, teeth, the cranium of an infant chalked with mystical symbols. A crown he wore, a cap of grave-gold patterned with chevrons and lozenges, and from it sprouted the bleached antlers of a stag, every tine whittled and thinned until it was sharp as a knife-blade.

"Who...who are you?" Isabella gasped. "Or what...?"

"I am the frost that nips, the river that claims a life, the ice that breaks beneath the skate. I am both old and young, acorn and oak. I saw the moon-eye when it first rose in the sky, I felt the sun's first glory undiminished. My people, whom you call 'Fae' or 'Elf' were the first people; the children of stardust. We were happy...till man came to blight the earth with his folly." His upper lip curled in a sneer. "Man with his pollution, his ignorance, his ugliness. We should have triumphed over such beasts, but instead they triumphed over us with their cold iron."

Grief filled the Elf's voice, a grief so deep that Isabella winced, but she shook her head. "We who live today at Elvingstone have never harmed you; any wrongs that were done to your people happened long ago"

"To me, an immortal, that time it but an eye's blink," sneered the Elf. "And the crimes of those who 'own' this land are legion, and not all in ancient times. Mine own sister, Blodeyn, went to the bed of a mortal and paid dearly for it."

"So did Augustus!" cried Isabella. "Floralie was not averse to the union; rather, it seemed to me she was willing, if not the instigator!"

"Augustus Stannion was a fool and aimed too high. Now his world will come crashing down...Forever!"

"You...you mean to kill me?" Isabella's heart thundered in her ears but she did not move and glared at the Elf-King defiantly. Running from him would be worse; he would send his wolf to tear her to shreds. "Go on, then, if it is your pleasure to attack a defenceless woman. Get it over with and stop toying with us!"

"Oh, I have no intention of killing you," said the Elf-King in a silken voice. "We of the Elfinkind are...attracted to humans, for all their barbarity and earthly grossness." He caught her hand, lifted it before his face, her wrist turned towards his face. For a moment, Isabella thought he was going to kiss her wrist but instead, he eyed the vein hungrily as if about to sink his teeth into it. She did not know which horrified her more.

"It is your warm red blood that attracts," he said. "If the Elfin folk once tumbled from heaven like stars, you humans crawled from the earth like maggots. We are high above you, and yet and yet...the scent of blood and soil and decay enthrals."

Suddenly his wiry arms were about her, pressing her against his glowing torso. Isabella smelt autumn leaves, smoke and winter. She smelt spring grass and flowers, the Rhododendrons of the Paladin's Rower—the Rhododendrons that never bloomed in late October.

Shuddering, she gazed up into the Elf-King's face, impossibly beautiful in its icy perfection. Eyes greener than moss stared down at her; eyes more brilliant that the gems in the crowns of mortal Kings. His pale lips, sensual without softness, parted to reveal strong white teeth. "Kiss me, Isabella Lawrence," he said, his voice a lure, a snare, musical but dark, its undertone racing wind, the wild thunder, the rain in the night. "Cleave to me, mind and body, and no harm will come to you. I swear this by the oaths of my people. You have come through time; I know of you; you are different from these others around you, more perfect, filled with the knowledge of the future. You belong with us, the Fae...not the earth-bound clods of city and town. I even give you my name—Iar, as proof of my good intentions—no small gift to reveal one's true name." He chuckled; it was the sound of icicles clacking on the roofline in midwinter. "Come with me under the hill and dance with me for all eternity. You were a dancer once, were you not?"

"That was Arabella Lorne, who my spirit...soul...or whatever jumped into," she said boldly. "I am as clumsy as fuck in my real life and have no wish to do the tango, horizontal or otherwise with you. I am Augustus's wife. All I want now upon this earth is to be with him, in peace. I do not desire anything you can offer me, Iar. Not you, not your eternity, not your magic...not even a return to my own time. That life is over. I want only for you to free me, and my husband who has become dearer to me than anything in the world. Your faery glamour will never tempt me."

King Iar's eyes flashed green fire. "It is too late for any compromise, any forgiveness. The Stannions must be abolished; no seed of theirs allowed flourishing." His green, piercing gaze slid down to her flat belly. "I could make you dance, Isabella who is also Arabella; dance until your feet turn to bloody stumps."

He snapped his long fingers, chill as icicles, and to her horror, Isabella felt her feet start to move. Her limbs tingled. Her arms lifted and she did a graceful pirouette upon the grass. Giddily, she spun in circles, hair flying, unable to stop, unable to fight back against the Elf-King's sorcery.

Iar snapped his fingers again. Isabella collapsed to the ground as if she were a puppet cut loose from its strings. She tried to crawl away, but Iar pursued her, laughing darkly.

The Elf-King bent over and lifted her up in his arms, almost tenderly—but in his austere face, his eyes were harder than diamonds. "See, little Isabella. I can control your body. Any aspect of it."

His mouth touched hers; an icy kiss, without passion, but all about possession and domination. Her teeth ached with the coldness of him and she struggled to free herself from his unwanted embrace, pounding his chest with hands clenched into tight fists. Iar looked surprised, as if he had expected his attentions would be welcomed.

"Let go you me, you bastard!" she raged. "And don't look so shocked—I am not some wilting Victorian flower stricken by the vapours. I took self defence!"

Noticing his hesitation, Arabella reached down and yanked off one of her shoes. A stupid weapon, seemingly of little effect against this great, otherworldly lord, and yet...yet there was something about it, something that made it special....

A sturdy metal, painted silver to hide its workaday grey hue, capped the spike of the little, daggered heel.

It was iron, deadly to the Fae folk of the Otherworld.

Iron.

"Get away from me, you monster!" warned Arabella, brandishing the shoe as if it were a sword. "I know the weakness of your kind; you spoke of it yourself. You fear iron...and it can kill faery folk, like it killed Augustus's son. Take a step back from me, Iar, or believe me, I will ram this iron spike into one of those pretty emerald eyes of yours."

Gaze fixated on the deadly iron spike, Iar hissed in anger, his tongue thrusting serpent-like between his lips. The tip was forked. "You have the better of me this night, Isabella Lawrence, but the Elves of Elvingstone have won the day, nonetheless. We have subdued Augustus Stannion and carried him into the faery hill, where he will shed his blood as a tithe to the forces of what mortals name 'Hell' in the Christian Holy Book. Thus shall he atone for the wrongs of his family toward the Fae, and for his own misdoings."

"You are monsters, vengeful monsters!" Isabella screamed at the Elf-King, the iron-spiked shoe still in her upraised hand. "I will not let you do this! To save Augustus, I will follow him to Hell itself if need be, I swear it!"

Iar's lips curled in a mocking smile. "Such a fierce cat, Isabella/Arabella! Your claws must be cut. I trust we will meet again soon, and upon my territory, where your little shoe with its button of iron will be of limited protection. You will dance with me, on the Elfin dance floors...and in my bed. You will soon forget that fool, Augustus Stannion!"

He whirled around, the bones fastened to his necklace clacking, and became a tall, spiralling whirlwind of light. Rising from the ground, Iar of Elvingstone flew with all speed towards St Michael's church and his lair in the churchyard beyond.

The white wolf growled and stared at Isabella with a hungry glance. Dropping to its belly, it began to crawl towards her, saliva dripping from its jaws.

"Go with your master; get away from me!" Desperately Isabella swung out at the wolf with her shoe. The spiked heel struck the beast's nose, biting deep into the sensitive flesh. Green blood spewed across the lawn and an acrid smoke arose, burning Isabella's eyes.

The wolf yelped and started to run in circles, smoke pouring from its nose and fur. Seconds later, its shape shimmered like sunlight on water and it turned into a twisted, rat-like creature, hairless and ashen-pale. Squealing loudly in fright and pain, it shot past Isabella and darted into the bushes.

Isabella stared after the creature, trying to control her wild breathing and racing heart. Then she kicked off her remaining shoe, and dragging her skirts to the knee, uncaring of Victorian modesty, she flew on bare feet towards the grand stone bulk of Elvingstone Manor.

The great hall of the manor house was in disarray. Decorations for the Ball lay strewn across the floor, tables were overturned, a chandelier hung at an odd angle. The air was thick with hazy blue smoke and reeked of sulphur. Servants milled about in a stunned state, trying to comfort each other. Weeping furiously, face red and swollen, Jemima was huddled behind an upturned chair.

In the middle of the floor sprawled a hideous creature, slightly shorter than the average man, with scaly grey lizard skin and gnarled tusks sprouting from its jaw. Great, yellow, lamp-eyes glared sightlessly at the ceiling. A reeking blood-red cap lay beside the monster's head, tangled with tendrils of matted grey hair. A rusty billhook lay beside a clawed hand. At the centre of the monster's forehead was a wide bullet-hole; viscous blood oozed from it, while a thin column of smoke rose from the wound.

"Oh, Mistress, Mistress!" Clambering to her feet, Jemima stumbled to Isabella's side. "I am so glad you are here! It was awful. Awful! We couldn't help the Master, and now he's gone."

Isabella clawed at the girl's shoulders, rough in her own desperation. "Jemima, tell me what happened. Hold nothing back."

Jemima wiped at her face. "We were just having a nice time, serving drinks and dinner, when we heard shouting. Looking out, we saw the sky had turned a funny colour and felt a coldness in the air—ate into the bones, it did! Master Augustus came flying up to the house with a pistol in hand; he was looking around him wildly. Out of the topiary garden marched four foul…creatures…" She aimed a shaky kick at the sprawled corpse on the floor. "All of them the same as that dead one, armed and ready to kill and maim."

"Do you know what they are, Jemima?" asked Isabella. "I will not pretend I know of these beings in the way you and Nanny do."

"Yes, Mistress! They call them Red Caps; the guards of the Elf-King. They like to live in old, ruined towers. They dye their caps in the blood of slaughtered men."

"What did they do when they appeared? And what…what did Augustus do?" Isabella swallowed, trying to contain her roiling emotions. Half of her wanted to grab a gun or sword and go rushing after these creatures…but that would help no one.

"They fell upon the Master by the front door, while behind them stood that termagant, Floralie, eager to vent her wrath on him. She laughed as the Red Caps slashed at him with their weapons; sulked when he avoided their blows. He shot at one and missed; then he shot at Floralie herself but she vanished like the morning mist, even as he pulled the trigger. Seeing he was outnumbered, he ran into the hall and shouted that we bar the doors. It was too late. The Red Caps forced their way in, smashing up the furniture and beating us out of the way. Pearl has a black eye and Carver's nose is broken.

Seeing the creatures assailing Sir Augustus, the last partygoers fled in terror, some even jumping out through the windows. The Master fired his last bullet at one of the Red Caps and the beast fell down dead, just as you see him." She kicked at the fallen Red Cap again. "His death did not halt his fellows, though; they tore the pistol from the Master's hands and took him prisoner, threatening him with their bills. I screamed like a demon, Mistress Arabella— I thought they'd hack him limb from limb before my very eyes. But no, once he was subdued, they dragged him towards the faery hill by the church."

Isabella buried her face in her hands. "It is exactly as Iar the Elf-King said; they have taken Augustus, seeking revenge for wrongs his family inflicted centuries ago. And for Floralie...and Aelfred. Oh, what fools we were to hold the Ball on All Hallows Eve, of all nights! Even in my day, some considered Halloween an 'unholy' time!"

"Eh, ma'am, not sure what you mean?" said Jemima, frowning in perplexity at Isabella's final statement. "What do you mean 'your day?"

"No time to explain!" Isabella said firmly and hastily. "I need to know how the Elves gained access to the Ball. We laid out salt and horseshoes as Nanny advised. You did put out the...the *other* offering, didn't you?" She peered at the maid with slight distrust. Who could she full trust in this place?

Jemima looked hurt. "'Course I did, mistress. I painted the doors of their horrible mound with it, afraid all the time that one of them would reach out and grab me. The problem was...the children. It was the children, Miss Arabella."

"Children? What children?"

The ones from the village, ma'am, that were invited to the Ball with their parents. They grew restless, as little ones often do, and went exploring the estate on their own. They found the horseshoes and took them as souvenirs, the horrible little beggars! I saw them waving them about in the gardens and shouted that they were to put them back at once, but before I could see that they obeyed, the Red Caps came out of the mound, singing:

"For want of a nail the shoe was lost.
For want of a shoe the horse was lost.
For want of a horse the knight was lost.
For want of a battle the kingdom was lost.
And all for the want of a horseshoe nail."

Jemima began to cry, wiping her face with her apron. "Ah, those silly little brats; they'd done for us all! If only their parents had taught them the old faery lore, but no, they say we are in the Age of Reason, and we should not teach such outdated foolishness to the younglings. Look where such blinkered views have landed us! Master Augustus is gone. We're ruined!"

"I must go." Murmuring to herself, Isabella turned away from the weeping Jemima. "I swore I would do it, and so I shall."

"Go? Where are going?" Jemima flicked a tear from the corner of her eye. "Are you leaving Elvingstone? Maybe that would be wise...maybe they are out to get you too..."

"Leaving?" Isabella stared at the maid in disbelief. "You underestimate me, Jemima! I'll never leave, not without Augustus. I am going to that blasted Elf hill…to get him back."

"You are…*what*?" cried Jemima, dismayed, throwing up her hands. Tears burst from her eyes again, runnelling down her plump cheeks. "No, no, this is madness…you mustn't go there! You cannot face them in their own domain! You will never be seen again. Where is Nanny? She will tell you."

"Nanny is in the summerhouse and has had one of her 'turns'; I dare say these spells of senselessness she suffers are caused by the Elf-King…by magic or hypnotism or something. She won't be of any help to us unless she recovers instantly. I don't have time to wait and see if she regains her wits. I must go alone. It is my duty to attempt to rescue my husband…or die in the attempt." A lump of sickness rose in Isabella's gullet—what was she saying? She sounded like a character in a TV show, full of noble sentiments…but real life wasn't so simple. She wanted to save Augustus, but in truth, she was terrified. Terrified. Rage and fear had made her speak to Iar with over-confidence. What could she really do against such a creature? A creature that shouldn't even exist!

Jemima's flushed face turned bone-white "Oh, Mistress Arabella, this madness is too much to bear. Please don't be a fool! A woman can't face them alone. You need an army behind you, and no one will listen. They'd put you in an institution!"

A woman can't face them…Isabella took a deep, shuddering breath. She couldn't believe that…after all, she'd grown up in the age of '*Girl Power*'! She might be scared witless, but if no one else were willing to help…she'd have to damn well help herself. And if she failed…she tried to block that awful outcome from her mind.

"Jemima, I don't have an army, but I am not as helpless as you seem to think. I…I am not just an actress. I have another history. I lived another life besides that of Arabella Lorne."

Jemima blinked. "Ma'am, I don't understand? Another life? Are you…some kind of foreign spy? Royalty in disguise? Some scandalous woman like that awful, brash writer Caroline Norton, who denied that her earnings and her children belonged to her husband?"

"You wouldn't believe me if I told you," said Isabella with a grim, tight smile. "Now stop wittering! Get me some riding breeches and a tight-fitting jacket. I cannot wear flouncing gowns if I am to battle for Augustus's life and freedom. And hurry up; we've wasted enough time in pointless chat! I hope it is not too late already!"

Looking stunned, Jemima scuttled out of the great hall and Isabella hurried into Augustus's smoking room. She took up one of his duelling pistols—no iron bullets, alas—and wrenched an ornamental, but sharp, sword from a display case on the wall. It had an iron blade, red with the rust of years.

Jemima bustled into the smoking room, puffing and gasping, with clothes slung over one arm. Dropping them on the back of Augustus's high-backed chair, she began to help Isabella out of her ball-gown. "I still wish you wouldn't do this, Mistress!" she wailed. "No matter if you *are* truly as wicked and unnatural as that Caroline Norton!"

"Jemima, just stop! Suffice it so say, if I am unsuccessful in my goal, my life here…means nothing. I would rather be a virago than a milksop. Maybe you, or your great, great, great granddaughters, if you ever have any, will realise that! Now quickly, help me change!"

Dressed in her breeches and riding habit, Isabella reached over her shoulder and scraped her long, thick hair into a rough braid for neatness. Then she thrust sword and pistol into her waistband and strode boldly across the great hall, past the cowering servants, past the reeking corpse of the slain Red Cap, down the Hall of Thrones and mirrors, and out into the night.

She had never felt so alone. What she faced was worse than any modern mugger, or even a terrorist. Gravel skittering beneath her shoes, she began to walk steadfastly towards St Michael's church, bathed in the tremulous light of that wicked, skull-faced moon which had ridden the heavens all night like a sinister genie upon a carpet of ragged cloud.

The wind was cool, licking her face, but at least it smelt fresh, without the taint of the Otherworld, either fair or foul. Stars winked above in the hard vault of the sky, one of the constellations forming a jewelled crown over the crenellated top of St Michael's church tower. The Stygian avenue of yews beckoned, their branches shuddering and rustling, leaning together like conspirators.

Taking a deep breath, she stepped between the knotted boles of the trees, fancying she saw shifting shapes skitter between the twisted roots. Instinctively her hand descended on the hilt of Augustus's old sword; her one slim comfort with its narrow iron blade. In all honesty, she felt no more intimidating that a pantomime pirate with a plastic cutlass…

A dozen paces…then several steps. *One. Two. Three…* To her relief, she was through the muddy yew-lined lane, past the trickling waters of the Holy Well, and facing the gate that opened into the disused part of the cemetery. Trying to keep her hand from trembling, she pushed the gate open. Hinges squealed like a soul in torment, making her jump; the sound seemed as loud as a scream in the silence. Slowly, the gate drifted open to admit her to the enclosure and hung there, creaking in the wind.

With tentative steps, Isabella stepped over the threshold into the graveyard. All was still, seemingly peaceful. Moths fluttered in the gloom, wings vibrating and making a soft whirr as they tangled in her hair; glow-worms cast muted light-trails around the leaning tombstones.

The Stannion vault—the Elfin hill—stood in dark silhouette against the bluish background of the night sky. The unmown grasses covering the tumulus whispered in the wind; on its summit, the mournful stone angel stood eternal, hands pressed together in prayer, staring up at the unyielding heavens. A glow-worm crawled along her cheek; night-dew wet the hollows of her carven eyes. Mere inches beneath her marble toes, the red, rusted doors to the inner vault stood shut, the padlock dangling down and rattling in the breeze. The remains of Jemima's blood offering smeared the corroded metal like a set of obscene hieroglyphics.

Despite the forays of the Fae into the mortal world, the Stannion crypt looked as if no one had opened it for a hundred years or more…

"I am coming for you, Augustus," Isabella murmured. "I know you are in there…with them."

She drew the pistol from her waistband, aimed it carefully. Inwardly, she gave thanks that she had learned to fire a gun while visiting her uncle's farm in Devon. Her mother had disapproved and berated Uncle George no end for putting his ten-year-old niece in 'danger.' Isabella had quite enjoyed the experience but dared not say so; she had never shot a real gun again, but had learned a good aim from summertime paintball competitions with her work colleagues…

Slowly, she squeezed the trigger on Augustus' old pistol. The gun went off with a flash and a roar. The bullet tore into the large, heavy padlock and shattered it. Broken shards thudded to the ground. The way to the Otherworld was open.

Isabella ran to the crypt and flung her full weight against the doors. Resistance…but not that much. She needed something to pry the doors open.

Groping around on the ground, she found a broken branch, which had fallen from a nearby dead bush. She thrust it into the crack between the doors and managed to jimmy them apart an inch or two. The doors were still unwilling to open further, and as she pressed her eye to the slender crack she'd made, Isabella could see fallen bricks from a sagging ceiling blocking the entrance to the crypt.

Using strength she did not know she had, Isabella kicked heartily at the base of the doors whilst twisting her stick in the crack until it seemed likely to snap in two. Slowly, moss, bricks and heaped grave-earth began to give way and suddenly the left door flew inwards, tearing away from one of its corroded hinges. Rank air reeking of dead things and stagnation rushed out of the sepulchre.

Coughing as unwholesome odours clawed the back of her throat, Isabella lit a taper after some minutes fussing with an old-fashioned strike-a-light and entered the mound. Beyond was a small oval room that seemed to have been some kind of funerary chapel. It had a blue tiled ceiling and floor, and a tarnished metal cross above what might have been an altar, now merely a crumpled pile of rotted wood. Past the altar, stretched a long tunnel winding into the body of the hillock.

Isabella proceeded down the corridor, hand pressed against the slimy wall to keep her balance in the gloom. Her taper only sent out a thin circle of light, quickly swallowed by the rancid darkness. However, as her eyes began to adjust to the dimness, she could see a number of wooden shelves with coffins upon them. Dust lay over them like a shroud, and spider webs formed lacy canopies. Some of the older coffins had fallen to the ground, their wooden trestles rotted away, and bones were strewn about the tunnel. Pates green with moss, skulls grinned at her amidst the detritus of centuries.

Gritting her teeth against the fear that threatened to overwhelm, she pushed on further. The passageway was narrowing, drawing to an abrupt close. A wall loomed up, blank and featureless. Isabella's heart sank. She could see nothing on the face of the wall that might indicate there was an entrance to a concealed part of the hill. Maybe the sorcery of the Fae obscured such a portal from human eyes; she simply did not know.

Lump in her throat, she poked disconsolately at a stack of coffins against the back wall. One hung open, the coffin lid wrenched from its hinges to reveal a white-clad female body, partly mummified, its bleached-out tresses permeating the chinks in the coffin. The mouth gaped in a silent, eternal scream, despite the strip of decayed linen binding the chin, and charnel remains of a bouquet of flowers lay upon the sunken chest. The light of Arabella's taper fell upon the brass nameplate affixed to the splintering wood. *Daria Harcourt, beloved of Aldous Stannion the Elder 1696.Rest Ye Gentle, Good Ladye.*

Isabella stared down at the pathetic heap of bones, all that remained of a mistress of one of the Stannions of long ago. At one time, she would have fled in a panic at what she beheld, even though she knew, as a modern woman, that the dead could not hurt you, only the living. Fear of the dead seemed ingrained in every living being, from the prehistoric eras onwards.

But now…her travel through time and her brief, strange, unexpected marriage to Augustus had brought out the steel in her soul. Or iron. She had witnessed the seemingly impossible, time travel, and now creatures out of legend and myth that spoke to her as any earthly human might. She had seen lakes turn to ice before her eyes; she'd suffered injury from a poisoned thorn. Old bones, no matter how grotesquely and irreverently arranged, would not deter her from her quest.

"You will have to do better than that, you soulless monsters!" she shouted into the shadows. "I will find out where you are holding my husband! Floralie will not have him as her plaything!"

Crawling forward nearly on her knees, she thrust the coffin and its occupant aside with a great effort. In her rickety box, Daria Harcourt and her flowers crumbled to dust. However, another coffin lay before Isabella, jammed up against the wall.

The sight of this one, however, made her utter a despairing moan. Although firmly closed, it was clearly a child's coffin fashioned from polished dark wood. The nameplate on the side was covered in graven scrollwork and one name stood out under a drawing of a winged cherub— *Aelfred.*

Augustus' young son, dead through his elfin blood and the power of cold iron.

This final manipulation of the dead was, Isabella guessed, a deliberate taunt, a stab at the heart by the unfeeling faery people. But was there more to it than that? Perhaps someone had moved these two coffins not only so that they would be seen as she approached the far end of the crypt, but for another purpose? What if they had been arranged to *hide* something?

Kneeling in a tangle of cobwebs, she pushed aside the small, pitiful coffin of Aelfred as dust showered, threatening to make her sneeze. Behind the casket, on the surface of the flat grey wall, she noticed a slender crack running through the stonework, rising to a peak near the ceiling, then running down the other side. Leaning forward, she let her finger trace the edge of the crack, knocking off a haze of dirt and damp mould. Right, up, down…the lines almost seemed to form the outline of a small, arched doorway.

Hopeful, she placed her shoulder against the cracked area of the wall, pushing at it to see if it would budge. Nothing happened. Impatient, stomach churning, she ran her finger over the crack again. Strangely, it seemed a little wider, the break in the stonework fractionally more prominent. Pressing her ear to the crack, she listened, and in the distance, heard noises one would never expect to hear underground: brazen horns and weird, exotic flutes, the clashing of chimes, the sound of high-pitched laughter and merrymaking.

"They are there!" she breathed triumphantly, and her head and heart were filled with thoughts of Augustus, as the Elves' prisoner, subject to the torments of his former wife, Floralie. Given as a tithe to hell. The thought spurred her to action. It was now or never.

"Let me through!" she suddenly screamed in desperation, pounding the wall with her fist until blood flowed. Blood, that thing desired and craved by the denizens of the faery realm. "I told you I would come for Augustus. He belongs in the mortal world and he has suffered enough at your hands. The sins of his ancestors should not be visited upon him. And you, Floralie, if you can hear me; you know he never intended to kill his son. If he did wrong, it was through his own ignorance, not malice. He loved Aelfred, and he loved you too—more fool him! The malice is all on your side! At least admit that, you unnatural bitch!"

The laughter and music within the hollow heart of the hillock ceased abruptly. An ominous silence and stillness descended over the mound.

A cold sweat broke out on the back of Isabella's neck. She did not know what was happening, but she knew without a doubt that something untoward was afoot, despite the stillness. Tension built up until the air crackled with it.

Then she heard a sound, a rushing like wind. Wind trapped within this vaulted place. Wind where no wind should ever have been able to blow. Wind from the Otherlands, from the Deadlands. It seeped through the cracks in the wall, buffeting her, driving her back down the corridor, and with the gusts came a green, unearthly light, witchfire that crept through the damaged stonework and illuminated the wrecked coffins, the fallen bones in their nests of spiders' webs.

The light shot upwards, clinging to the roof like a living thing, while the scent of sulphur permeated the air. In the distance, deep underground, hooves began to thunder, making the paving stones beneath Isabella's feet tremble then heave upwards, revealing masses of worms and serpents, slithering, knotting and looping together, wreathed in a horrible, phosphorescent glow.

Panic washed over Isabella in waves as she heard the hooves. She had not expected such a sudden and violent response. Indeed, she did not know exactly what she *had* expected from the Elves of Elvingstone—a one-on-one confrontation with their King or with Floralie? A war of words rather than weapons?

The urge for self-preservation dissolved her newfound courage in one fell swoop. She would be ridden down, trampled into the grave-mould if she remained where she was. Whipping around on her heels, she began to run at full tilt down the buckling corridor. Stone slabs leapt up around her, jutting like swords; skulls bounced and rolled, streaming verdigris; coffins and their contents split like disgusting over-ripe fruit, releasing acrid odours of ancient death.

At length, beyond all hope, she reached the corroded doors and the fresh air of the outside world. Tripping over the threshold, she fell to her knees on the damp path outside. Gasping in pain, she struggled around and tried to slam the doors shut, but remembered, with a sinking heart, that her pistol-shot had shattered the padlock—she could not lock the doors against the Fae.

Inside the hill, the thundering of hooves grew louder and louder. Suddenly, a great force struck the doors from behind, hurling her backwards onto the dew-drenched grass. Winded, she lay upon the ground, staring up at the hollow hill with the angel perched on top, looking mournfully and hopelessly at an uncaring heaven.

The doors were blown outwards, tearing completely from their hinges and clanging to the ground. Brazen trumpets blew into the night as a company of Elves rode from their secret underground lair into the world of men.

It seemed impossible that a whole troupe could emerge from one small hillock, but then such creatures, according to the learned, sensible men of the great universities of Arabella's day and to the scientists and sceptics of Isabella's, should not have existed to begin with. But they did, for they stood before her in their terrible splendour, and they were free in the world to do as they pleased.

Iar appeared, riding on a many-legged, ash-pale horse, the antlers on his crown embracing the waning moon above. At his side rode his sister Floralie, or Blodeyn, gowned in white samite and glowing like a fallen, dead star, her coiled hair tangling to her waist and the finger-bones of dead men, of long gone lovers, of hapless, besotted victims, bound to her girdle of pale mound-gold. A dagger was thrust into that belt; ancient, bronze, its hilt studded with golden pins. Around both Elfin siblings gathered the Host of the Air—warriors as tall as spears, glowing like lamps—a green knight wreathed in leaves, a sky-blue swordsman with hair of cloud, a sun-spearman spewing heatless orange flame from eyes and mouth and long, snarled tresses. They circled round Isabella on their Night-Mare steeds, cutting off any route to escape, sneering and mocking.

"Tonight is All Hallows," intoned the Iar, "the old Feast of Samhain, that holy night when the gates between the world of mortal and Elfinkind part. A night when our people ride out to pay a tithe to the Lords of the Infernal

Regions—Asmodeus, Orobas and others who wait in the pits of Everlasting Torment. Without the offering, the Fae would be sent to serve those Lords in Hell, since the One who created us has turned his face from us forever. But we are people of the Middle World, between Heaven and Hell, and want only to serve our own kind, as we have done for aeons. We do not wish to kneel before an infernal master."

"And so the offering to Hell will be made!" Floralie rose in her ornamental stirrups, hair a banner behind her in the breeze. "The fairest and youngest of all my Elfin knights!"

She gestured behind her and a pair of Red Caps marched from the hollow hill flanking a tall figure wearing a long robe the colour of new-shed blood. The figure's head was bowed, the neat dark hair held back by a silver fillet decorated with thorns that scored the white brow. The eyes were downcast and seemed unfocused in the pale, handsome face.

It was Augustus Stannion.

"Augustus!" Isabella cried, unnerved by his wan appearance and strange attire, willing him to wake from his stupor and look at her.

He did not glance up, seemed not to have heard her cry; he just stared at the ground while the Red Caps prodded him forward with the butts of their billhooks.

Floralie took the ancient dagger from her girdle and held it aloft in a shining fist. "Tonight his red, red blood shall run free. The sacrifice shall be made and my own vengeance taken. If Augustus Stannion is not with me, and we are sundered forever, I swear he will not be with any other, nor shall he prosper, nor flourish, nor indeed breathe any longer upon this earth. A human wrought from the clay must return to the clay." She smiled evilly, her fingers caressing the edges of the bronze weapon.

"You cannot do this to him!" Isabella flung herself toward the woman on her pale steed with its armour of bronze spikes. "How can you wish to murder him? You loved him once…you bore his child!"

"Love? You foolish humans are so obsessed by your talk of love. I did not 'love' him; my kind does not experience that weak emotion. I desired him to mate with, craved his bodily strength, savoured his beauty…that beauty which is so entrancing in mortal kind, for it fades and withers so fast, like the leaves that bloom on the trees each year. Beyond that…nothing, and then he brought war between us when his folly killed Aelfred."

Isabella gazed up at the shining figure with the dagger shining like a tear of the sun, beautiful yet deadly. The child; Floralie claimed her people hadn't the ability to love but yet she clearly she mourned her lost child. How could she say that her devotion to Aelfred, even if its tragic outcome had engendered hatred towards Augustus, was not born of maternal love?

"Floralie, you are a liar!" she said forcefully. "You loved Aelfred, if not any other of mortal blood; I do not doubt you cried tears for his passing, even if they were tears of ice! Was he to return from the realm of the dead, what would he think to see his mother sacrifice his own father upon All Hallows? Killing his own sire for a tragic accident that he never anticipated! You know what would happen then? Aelfred would fear his own unnatural mother and hate her forever for her cruelty and vengefulness!"

Floralie released an enraged scream and her eyes glowed hot as fire, red and demonic in the pristine mask of her face. Isabella's words had touched something fragile within her ice-cold heart. Tears began tracking down the curves of her cheeks; tears hard as diamonds and the colour of blood. "Speak to me of my son no more! No more! And if you desire Augustus Stannion so much, go to him, and take him…if you can!"

She waved her dagger in the direction of the Red Caps and they lowered their bills and retreated, leaving Augustus standing alone in his fillet of faery-gold. Slowly he raised his head and for an instant Isabella's heart leapt with hope…but then, when she gazed into his blue eyes, she found only emptiness, desolation, no recognition at all. It was as if he were a shell, with his soul, if such truly existed—imprisoned far away. Dead eyes.

"Augustus! Augustus!" Despite his lack of response, she ran to his side and flung her arms around him. He felt cold; through the thin fabric of his elfin robes, she could feel no normal human heart beat. That shocked her, made her feel ill…was he was walking dead man?

Nonetheless, Isabella clung to him, kissing his slack mouth, his vacant eyes, caressing the marble expanse of his brow, doing all she could to awaken him as if in a reverse story of Sleeping Beauty , where a princess woke the slumbering prince. "Augustus, I've come to take you home! Please, please, look at me; come back to me! I swear we can overcome this evil together! "

Augustus shuddered and bent his head towards hers. For a second, she thought he was about to kiss her, but to her horror he saw his dead eyes change, becoming hard black pebbles—the pitiless eyes of a serpent. He opened his mouth and a reptilian hiss emerged, along with a cloud of sulphurous mist that blasted into Isabella's face.

"No!" she screamed, refusing to let go of him despite her terror and revulsion. She clung to his sacrificial robe, her fingers knotting in the cloth until her knuckles glowed white. Before her horrified gaze, Augustus continued to transform, scales appearing on his limbs and a black tongue curling over teeth that were now needle-sharp fangs. Her husband had transformed into a huge, coiling serpent, cold-blooded and deadly, preparing to strike with venomous bite, or perhaps crush her to death.

Despite her fear, Isabella refused to relinquish her hold. Grimly she clung to the serpentine coils, avoiding the lash of the tail, the scoring of the fangs. "I know it is just Fae glamour, Augustus!" she cried out, as she was dashed to the ground, the serpent's coils rolling over her, pressing her down into the mud. "Even should you kill me tonight, the fault will never be yours but the fault of those who enchant you! I will never willingly let you go to them."

The serpent stopped writhing in her arms. The weight upon her, crushing, ceased. But there was only a minute's respite. Rearing away from her, the snake began to change appearance yet again—but not back to the man it had been. Instead, a lumbering black bear towered over Isabella, pummelling the star-streaked sky with huge claws. Throwing back its head, it uttered a bestial roar that sent night-birds sailing in fright from the avenue of yew trees toward the safety of the manor house.

Isabella lunged at the beast, throwing one arm around the thick neck and burying her face in the bristling pelt. The bear smelt of musk, dead fish and carrion, but underneath, if she pressed herself close enough, she could detect a faint trace of the scent Augustus always wore—vague but still tantalising, binding her to this powerful creature that threatened her existence.

"I will not let you go, Augustus," she repeated between clenched teeth as the bear attempted to swat her aside as if she were an annoying fly. "I know you would never willingly hurt me. If I come to harm, it is the fault of Floralie and the Elves. I swear I will save you from their devices, even if I must perish myself."

The bear roared again, as if in sudden pain, and it collapsed with a mighty thud, dragging Arabella to the ground with it. Swiftly its eyes glazed over while steaming saliva trickled from its jaws. Isabella crawled over to the beast, placing the limp head in her lap. "Augustus...Augustus?" She shook the massive ruff in alarm. The creature appeared...dead....its tongue lolling, the whites of its eyes showing. Fear spiked through her.

"No, no, you cannot be dead!" Desperately, she clutched the fur again, but to her shock, sections of pelt tore away in her hands.

With a cry of alarm, she toppled backwards, unbalanced. The carcase of the bear was disintegrating into a heap of ash, leaving only the tufts of fur in her hands, which in their turn were changing. The matted clumps were metamorphosing into a pair of red-hot coals.

Isabella shrieked in sudden pain as the coals burnt the palms of her hands. "Cast them from you, divest yourself of that which brings you agony!" she heard Floralie cry, voice harsh as the cawing of crows. "Otherwise, your fingers will be burnt to the bone, and for what? For a man? You have beauty—many men would gladly warm your bed. Abandon Augustus Stannion. He is the true cause of your suffering!"

"I will not!" wept Isabella, still defiant despite the searing pain. "I will hold onto these burning glebes as if they were precious jewels because that is how they seem to me, knowing that the essence of Augustus is in them. I would never cast him from me! Never!"

Floralie's visage took on a new expression, softer, pitying. "He will bring you nothing but grief, Isabella Lawrence. As he did to me. Pain of the body, pain of the heart. His is not of your time, just as he was not of my world. He is poison...to us both. Let me have him. For you...I can offer you passage to your old home..."

She breathed upon her palm; golden dust blew out in a vast cloud and formed a whirling vortex. In its heart, Isabella could see faint images— London black cabs and double decker buses, tourist crowds, Buckingham Palace, the London Eye, the Tower in all its stern splendour, Boudicca's Statue, the turrets of Westminster. Big Ben's face was like a shining eye, and out of a vast distance, the famous clock began to chime, its tones so familiar to Isabella. A stab of nostalgia and longing rushed through her.

"Go, jump into the heart of the whirlwind," enticed Floralie. "Do it now, for when the great clock strikes twelve, the way will be closed forever and you will never be able to go home again. Go home, Isabella Lawrence, forget Augustus Stannion as part of a bad dream. That's all this night will seem to you—a dream."

For a moment, Isabella wavered. Safety, familiarity, security all beckoned. With a small cry, she reeled toward the glowing vortex. She was still carrying the burning coals.

"Drop them!" ordered Floralie, the imperious tone returning to her voice. "Just you!"

Isabella gazed into the heart of the whirling light once again. And suddenly she noticed something odd. London…was *different*. The buses were the wrong colour, and she remembered none of the adverts on their sides. The bends in the river seemed different and there was an unfamiliar castle on one shore. Tower Bridge was gone…and instead there was a medieval structure with towers that she assumed was long-gone *London* Bridge! Most tellingly of all, the hands of Big Ben were the wrong way round; the clock was running backwards…

It was a false depiction of London. A faery mirage.

"You've tried to deceive me!" Isabella cried. "That's not my home…that just a vision!"

Floralie screamed in rage and the vortex imploded in a shower of gold. "Burn then, you fool!" cried the Elfin princess. "Burn you hands and your heart to ash protecting that miscreant, Augustus Stannion!"

The coals in Isabella's hands grew even hotter. Her agony grew more intense; her stomach heaved and the world began to spin as she realised she could smell her own flesh burning. "I…I cannot hold…" She staggered forward, feeling the coals slide between tortured fingers.

A hand descended on her arm, giving it a firm and reassuring squeeze. Nanny Burtoncappe stood beside her, her faculties clearly restored once more, the beak of her nose protruding beyond the rim of her midnight-blue hood.

"Nanny!" cried Isabella, dismayed rather than relieved. Nanny had knowledge but she was clearly no match for the Fae. "Get away from here, get away. It's not safe. You must leave."

"No, child, you must listen to me and do as I say." Nanny seemed as calm as if she were merely advising her on a choice of gown or what to have for tea. "You must come with me at once. At once."

A howl of anger rose from the Elves and the tall warriors surged forward, drawing weapons from their belts. "No!" Nanny held up her hand and it seemed to Isabella, through her pain-wracked and heat-seared eyes, that light shone from a ring upon Nanny's finger, flashing into the faces of the Fae and driving them back towards the open crypt. "You have set her a task, and unless she fails utterly, you must allow her to complete it. You know that is The Law!"

Turning her back the Elves, she guided Isabella away from the mound, out of the creaking gate, and to the Rag Well, Lady's Well, which bubbled in its green trough in the lane near the enclosure wall. The clouties attached to the surrounding shrubs sailed like pale ghosts in the wind; the moon's wan light trembled on the dark water oozing from the core of the earth.

"They say baptism is a form of rebirth," Nanny said grimly. "Do what you feel is right, Arabella...Isabella. I can help you no more than that upon this hour, on this ill-starred day. Let your senses, and your love, guide you."

Isabella fell to her knees beside the Lady Well, onto stones deeply grooved where generations had knelt in supplication of the spirits of the pure, clean water. Her first instinct was to hurl the coals into the water, to free her body of the pain ripping through her being and causing her heart to leap and stutter. But she could not do it. Those coals, which maimed her palms, which slowly killed her, were all she had left of Augustus.

With a low moan of defeat, she plunged head first into the green swell of the waters, still clinging to the burning coals. Down, down, she sank, hair spinning out like a mandala across the surface of the water.

In her hands, the burning coals were extinguished. Her fingers started to unpeel from them. The charred black lumps spun away into the darkness and waving weeds, spiralling down into unknown depths. She had lost them.

She had failed.

Augustus was gone from her.

Tormented, she glanced down at the hands that had betrayed her at the last, tentatively flexing each finger, forcing herself to witness the devastation of her flesh.

There were no burns.

All traces of burnt, seared skin had vanished. All was as it had been before All Hallows night. On her perfect, unmarred fingers, her wedding band and the ring Augustus had given her at the theatre glowed with a warm, mellow luminescence.

She began to cry, her tears mingling with the chilly waters of the Lady Well.

Then she stopped.

Something was travelling at speed towards her through the bubbling spring, something pale green, white and silver that arrowed towards the well's surface as if it was a shooting star trapped beneath the water. Alarmed she jolted away, but then her hands were caught, encased in other hands, human hands....Augustus's hands.

In shock, she pulled back, her hands knotted with her husband's in an unbreakable grip. Gasping, Isabella and Augustus collapsed in a heap together on the edge of the Lady Well, below the fluttering clouties, symbols of hopes and wishes.

"Augustus, oh God, Augustus!" Isabella sat up first, pulling his inert form towards her, showering his face with kisses. Slowly Augustus opened his eyes, and now they held both life and knowledge. And love for the woman who held him, there upon the dew-drenched grass near Lady Well. "Where am I? I...I cannot remember. You were hurt; I...I shot that creature..."

"You are safe now, safe." Isabella bent closer to him, trying to shield him from the hostile stares of the Elves, who gathered near the gate, watching with the eyes of serpents. She did not know if he truly was, but she would not tell him otherwise. If they were both to die, he would at least die in the knowledge that she was with him, protecting him.

Nanny Burtoncappe, who had watched from the shadows, stepped jauntily toward the faerie troupe. "Go now!" she ordered. "She has passed the tests as prescribed. You have lost your sacrifice. You have done enough evil to this family, and to me, their loyal servant and guardian. So depart, and come not here again."

"You meddlesome old hag! I will punish you for your interference." Floralie spurred her spectral steed forward, her eyes crackling fury, but her brother, King Iar, reached out an arm and jerked her back viciously, nearly unseating her.

"No," he thundered, his face impassive as a barren mountainside. "The mortal passed the tests and has won her lover's freedom. It is Law we let them pass unharmed. You have lost us the Tithe, Blodeyn, my foolish, jealous sister. You know what that will mean for us!"

Blodeyn's wrathful expression changed instantly to one of terror. "The Darkness will feast upon us if the Tithe is not paid. The One who sits on High will not accept the people of the Middle Kingdom, but the daemons in Hell will gladly bathe us in the Lake of Fire for eternity. Forgive me, my brother! Forgive me!"

"Forgive you?" The antlered King snarled. "Never until the world is ended! For your folly, Blodeyn, you will pay the Tithe yourself!"

In an unexpected move, he spurred his horse at Isabella, but not in an attempt to ride her and Augustus down. Instead, he snatched the iron sword from Isabella's belt and swinging round, thrust it up to the hilt in Blodeyn's white-clad breast.

The Elves of Elvingstone began to shriek and wail in despair. Whirlwinds arose, speckled with lights, engulfing their forms, which began to lose both shape and substance. Only the Elf-King stood out from the others, mounted on his eight-legged steed, with the languid body of Floralie draped over his arm, her green elfin heart's blood spilling from her bosom, mingling with the black waterfall of her unbound hair.

Behind them, the elf-hill, the ancestral Stannion crypt, emitted a deep groan, as if all the souls of those buried within breathed out in relief, and seconds later, its summit collapsed, falling inwards with a deafening roar. Earth-clods and timeworn brick tumbled; the angel memorial stood atop the wreckage for a moment, teetering on its plinth, then it hurtled to the earth with sickening impact, the head shattering and wings snapping off.

As dust began to settle, the Elves ceased their frenzied shrieking and changed to mere Will o' the Wisps, noisome as corpse-candles, that were blown out of the churchyard on the rising breeze.

It was over.

Augustus Stannion staggered to his feet, gazing at the shattered ruins of the tomb. "They are gone...the Elves of Elvingstone are gone, truly gone. Can you not feel it?"

"Yes, yes," breathed Isabella, clinging to his hand. "The air...It is fresher, and there is lightness in everything around us. Even though the sun is not up, there is no true Darkness here anymore!"

"You have saved me." He raised a shaking hand to touch her cheek, stained with dirt and tears. "In so many ways. And to think, I at one time wanted you only to stand in for *her*, a poor imitation. I was so wrong, so foolish and deceived. She was the one who was an imitation, parodying what should be most important in a man's life."

"Let's never speak of her again." Isabella fell into his embrace, and they held each other beneath the failing, fading moon with the dawn wind around them, breathing new life into old, decaying Elvingstone. "There is no need. She is gone and we are free to live our lives. To...to be as man and wife unimpeded. To be Master and Mistress of Elvingstone Manor to the end of our days." Suddenly she shuddered and pressed herself even closer to him. "Oh, when I thought I had lost you, it was as if I had entered the darkest Hell, the ones the Elves feared. I would have followed you there, you know, if it had been asked of me."

"I worship you for your bravery. And I love you as I never thought I would love a mortal woman."

Standing to one side, Nanny Burtoncappe fiddled with her bonnet and cleared her throat. "The morning star is up and it is near enough cock's crow. I think it is best we all get back to the manor, to have some nice, comforting tea and get some proper rest!"

The golden-cased clock in Augustus Stannion's smoking room ticked noisily. The Master of Elvingstone glanced at it and made a small, annoyed clicking noise between tongue and teeth. "Where the devil is that doctor?" he murmured.

Almost as if on cue, a small, burly man with a handlebar moustache poked his head through the open door. He carried a battered medical bag under one arm. "Sir Stannion," he said, "I have checked your wife thoroughly and she is in fine form despite the accident you described. No harm has come to her; there is no sign of any wound on her arm, none at all. Maybe it was all women's hysteria, brought on by the troubles of that night. Her vital signs are good and her health seems excellent." Suddenly he doffed his round bowler cap and chewed on the end of his moustache, looking both embarrassed and perplexed. "One thing I must ask, though, Sir Augustus..."

"What is it, Dr Mabbott?" Impatiently Augustus quirked an eyebrow. "Is there something else you've found wrong with my wife other than possible 'hysteria'?

"No, sir. And my question is not about Mistress Stannion. I wanted to ask you about the Ball. I didn't attend; I was out delivering Mrs Farrell's new twins down in the village. But I heard repeated stories about rum goings on; spirits and monsters chasing folk and the like. Now I am a thinking man, a doctor of medicine, as you know; I've had a decent education. I do not believe in such nonsense. But when dozens say similar things..." Mabbott shrugged and stared uneasily down at his shoes.

"Spirits and monsters!" Augustus said scornfully. "All that happened was a sudden fierce wind. A whirlwind. A small tornado. Rare, in this country, but not unheard of. It took down the party decorations, sent them flying into people's faces. Then Mistress Stannion had her accident, nicked her arm on broken glass and fell into a faint, and I took her to the summerhouse to lie down. When I was inside, I heard screaming and when I looked out, people were running like scared rabbits. I think their imaginations got the better of them. Maybe they saw some marsh-gas over the lake, I don't rightly know."

"Maybe, Sir Stannion." Dr Mabbott looked doubtful. "But some folk working in the house claim to have seen..."

"Mass hysteria, then," said Augustus curtly. "Isn't that a thing spoken of by head-doctors? Hysteria. You said yourself my wife might have suffered that malady. You won't encourage tales of ghosts and goblins, will you, Doctor?"

The stout little man shook his head.

"Well, then...a good day to you, Dr Mabbott."

The butler escorted the doctor out, and Isabella and Nanny appeared in the corridor outside the smoking room. Isabella was wearing a ruffled rose-hued dress, with her hair primly pinned up; she now looked every inch the lady of the manor, not the breeches-wearing fighter who had defied the Elves of Elvingstone.

"Everything is fine," she said, entering the room squeezing her husband's hand. "I told you it would be. My family are tough; I am tougher than I look. I won't shatter like glass."

"Thank heavens all is well, that is all I can say." He drew her to him in a rough but loving embrace.

"So all's well that ends well, as the old saying goes," said Nanny, with a toothless grin.

"And for that, we owe you so much, Nanny, with all your knowledge of the Elves and their ways," said Isabella, earnestly. "You saved us...many times, and probably more than we know about. I think you should be rewarded in some way; don't you, Augustus?"

"Of course. Nanny's knowledge of the Elfinkind has proved invaluable time and time again. What would you like, Nanny? Name it and it's yours."

Nanny knitted her spindly fingers together. "I ask but one thing—that I be godmother to the babe when it is born."

"What 'babe'?" asked Isabella, bemused. "Are you predicting something, Nanny?"

"Not at all, dear…but you are two healthy, married, young people. I expect the nursery will be full before long!"

"Well, if you wish to be godmother to any future Stannion children, I will gladly grant your wish," said Isabella. "You were godmother to many Stannions in the past, weren't you?"

"Indeed," Nanny replied, eyes glinting in her depths of her hood. "It was almost a regular duty until Floralie arrived at Elvingstone and broke the protective circle. I am so pleased the tradition will now be upheld. After all, what heir or heiress would not want a faery godmother to look over them?"

Isabella stared at her with widening eyes. "Yes, Isabella," the old woman leaned over and whispered in her ear. "I am *exactly* that. Not always kind but always clever and ready to defend my dear Stannions. It was I who guided your steps in the old Queen's Head and brought you through the centuries to meld forms with pretty, sprightly, but oh so vapid and humble Arabella Lorne. What do you say to that?"

"I say…" Isabella whispered back, "that you forget you told me. My life in the future has been erased. And don't call me by my old name anymore. I am…I will be in this age…Mistress Arabella Stannion."

Turning from Nanny, Isabella managed a wide smile. She extended a graceful gloved hand to her husband. "Let us go take the air, Augustus. I think it's going to be a fine day. A very fine day indeed."

THE END

If you have enjoyed this story, please check out my other works of historical fiction, historical fantasy and generic fantasy:

RICHARD III:

I, RICHARD PLANTAGENET-Tant Le Desiree Part 1.

The young Duke of Gloucester at Barnet and Tewkesbury. His fights with
George and married to Anne Neville. The Scottish campaigns.

I, RICHARD PLANTAGENET- Loyaulte Me Lie Part 2.

Kingship. The mystery of the Princes. The betrayal of Buckingham
and the

Stanleys. The final charge at Bosworth.

Omnibus Edition of I, RICHARD PLANTAGENET CONTAINING BOTH PARTS now available in Kindle and Print. Over 230,000 words!

A MAN WHO WOULD BE KING. The story of Harry Stafford, the treacherous Duke of Buckingham, who helped raise Richard III to the throne and then betrayed him. One of the suspects in the mystery of the Princes in the Tower.

SACRED KING.

Historical fantasy novella set at the time of Bosworth...and beyond. The afterlife of the King in the twilight realm of faerie...which Richard sees as Purgatory. A tale of hope and redemption, and of the finding of the long-dead King in a Leicester car park. A chance find...or not? The Return of the King.

WHITE ROSES, GOLDEN SUNNES.

Compilation of short stories (156 pages) of stories about Richard III and his family, frequently dealing with Richard's childhood and youth. Includes the tragic tale of his brother Edmund of Rutland.

MEDIEVAL:

MISTRESS OF THE MAZE. The story of Fair Rosamund, the mistress of Henry II. Captive in a bower, Henry sought to keep her safe from the wrath of Eleanor of Aquitaine.

MY FAIR LADY - A Story of Eleanor of Provence, Henry III's Lost Queen. First person fiction on the life of this half-forgotten Queen, who was the wife of Henry III, mother to Edward Longshanks...and one time regent of England. Set at the time of the second Barons' Revolt. An Amazon Best Seller in Historical Biographical Fiction and Medieval Historical Romance.

THE HOOD GAME- Historical fantasy about Robin Hood. Robin wins 'the Hood' in a dark and mystical rite, then if forced to take to the forest after killing a Norman knight.

KING ARTHUR/PREHISTORIC:

STONE LORD: The Legend of King Arthur. The Era of Stonehenge.
Britain, 1900 BC, the Great Trilithon at Stonehenge has been unruled for many years. Attackers seeking Britain's tin assail the shores. The shaman known as the Merlin seeks a youth who can draw the Sword from Beneath the stone and unite the warring clans. A retelling of the Arthurian legends with a prehistoric twist. Archaeology and legend combine.

MOON LORD : The Fall of King Arthur.The Ruin of Stonehenge.
Standalone sequel to STONE LORD. Ardhu the Great Chief's illegitimate son Mordraed comes to Kham-El-Ard to claim his birthright. A twisted youth with a face as fair as a god's but bearing a tormented heart, he wreaks terrible vengeance on his hated father by slaying, secretly, his half-brother, the otherworldy young warrior Gal'havad. Power growing, he then seeks to destroy Khor Ghor, the Giant's Dance on the Great Plain.

THE STONEHENGE SAGA-Omnibus containing both STONE LORD and MOON LORD

FANTASY:

BETWEEN THE HORNS: Tales From The Middle Lands.
Collection of humorous fantasy stories for all ages, set in a mythical central European country where each of the towns tries to out perform the others in its celebration of the seasons. A land between the Horn Mountains where giant hares lay eggs, trollocs dwell and the Krampus whips unruly children, where witches control the weather and look for fat boys to eat, and the Erl King rides in bleak midwinter. In the vein of Tim Burton.

MY NAME IS NOT MIDNIGHT
Dystopian fantasy set in a post apocalyptic 70's Canada. A young girl sets out on a quest to fight the religious oppression of the Sestren. In the vein of Philip Pullman.

Printed in Great Britain
by Amazon

70641630R00064